I'M TRAPPED IN
MY PRINCIPAL'S BODY

Other Books by Todd Strasser

Help! I'm Trapped in an Alien's Body

Help! I'm Trapped in Obedience School Again

Help! I'm Trapped in Santa's Body

Help! I'm Trapped in the First Day of Summer Camp

Camp Run-a-Muck series:

#1: Greasy Grimy Gopher Guts

#2: Multilated Monkey Meat

#3: Chopped Up Little Birdy's Feet

Help! I'm Trapped in My Sister's Body

Help! I'm Trapped in the President's Body

Help! I'm Trapped in My Gym Teacher's Body

Howl-A-Ween

Help! I'm Trapped in Obedience School

Abe Lincoln for Class President

Help! I'm Trapped in the First Day of School

Please Don't Be Mine, Julie Valentine

Help! I'm Trapped in My Teacher's Body

The Diving Bell

Free Willy (novelization)

Jumanji™ (novelization)

Home Alone™ (novelization)

Home Alone™ *II: Lost in New York* (novelization)

The Mall from Outer Space

HELP!
I'M TRAPPED IN
MY PRINCIPAL'S BODY

TODD STRASSER

AN
APPLE
PAPERBACK

SCHOLASTIC INC.
New York Toronto London Auckland Sydney

ISBN 0-590-12072-7

12 11 10 9 8 7 6 5 4 3 2   8 9/9 0 1 2 3/0

Printed in the U.S.A.   40

First Scholastic printing, September 1998

*To Geoff — who knows
what it's like*

1

"**H**ey, Jake," Alex Silver whispered. "How do you use *boycott* in a sentence?"

Our whole grade was in the cafetorium. It was the second week of school and we were taking some dumb state achievement test.

"*Shhh!*" I hissed back. "You're not supposed to talk."

"Come on, Jake, I haven't gotten one answer right so far," Alex whispered anxiously. "Just tell me."

"No!" I wiped some sweat off my brow. It was broiling hot in the cafetorium.

"How about you, Andy?" Alex whispered desperately. "Help me, *please*? I'm your friend. I mean, what are friends for? Come on, Andy."

"Cut it out, Alex," my friend Josh Hopka whispered hoarsely. "If you don't shut up, you're going to get us all in trouble."

"Tough," Alex grumbled and focused on Andy.

"I bet you know the answer, Andy. Just tell me and I'll shut up."

"Oh, okay, I'll give it to you, but just this one," Andy answered. "Girls sleep on a girlcott and boys sleep on a boycott."

Alex hesitated. "Are you *sure* that's the answer?"

"Pretty sure," Andy replied.

The cafetorium was filled with students. Our class was sitting together in the back. Teachers patrolled the aisles to make sure no one talked or shared answers.

"Andy," whispered Amanda Gluck. "What's the difference between electricity and lightning?"

"Can it, Amanda," Andy whispered back. "We're not supposed to share answers."

"You helped Alex," Amanda whined. "And it's just a state test. It's not like the grades count toward our report cards."

"Okay, Amanda, listen." Andy gave in. "I think it's that lightning's free, but you have to pay for electricity."

"Why didn't I think of that?" Amanda asked herself as she wrote down the answer.

"Hey, Andy," Barry Dunn muttered. Barry was a big guy with short blond hair and two earrings. He was the class bully and he loved picking on my friends and me.

"What do *you* want, Barry?" Andy whispered back, annoyed.

2

"I gotta use the word *tariff* in a sentence," Barry said. "Help me."

"Sure," Andy answered. "How about this? I'd rather drop dead than help you use *tariff* in a sentence."

"If you don't help me, you *will* drop dead . . . as soon as this test is over," Barry threatened.

Andy gave Josh and me a dismal look. We knew Barry meant it.

"Okay, here you go." Andy said with a defeated sigh. "Your pants are so tight they'll tariff you bend over."

"*Ha-ha!*" Amber Sweeny laughed out loud. Amber had long brown hair and was one of the prettiest girls at Burt Itchupt Middle School. She was also the smartest kid in our grade.

"What's with you?" Andy asked her.

"All your answers were totally wrong," Amber whispered.

"Are you serious?" Alex Silver gasped.

"You really believe a boycott is something you sleep on?" Amber replied.

"I *knew* that didn't sound right!" Alex mumbled. "Thanks a *lot*, Andy."

"Hey, I was only trying to help," Andy whispered back. "Besides, if you thought it didn't sound right, why'd you use it?"

"What about a tariff?" Barry Dunn asked Amber. "Was Andy wrong about that, too?"

"Did you say something, Barry?" a voice asked

behind us. Everyone went silent. It was our principal, Mr. Blanco. He was a short, pudgy man with curly hair. He usually wore a dark suit, but it was really hot and he'd taken off his jacket. His white shirt had large, dark sweat stains under each arm.

"Uh, no, Mr. Blanco," Barry replied. "I didn't say nothing."

"That's odd, Barry," Principal Blanco said as he patted some perspiration off his forehead with a handkerchief. "I distinctly heard you say something to Amber about a tariff. Now why would you say something like that?"

Barry didn't answer. Instead, he glared at Andy and narrowed his eyes in a menacing way. I knew what that look meant. It meant Barry had decided this was all Andy's fault. And if Andy didn't come to Barry's rescue fast, he was going to get beaten into a pulp.

"I think you may have heard wrong, Mr. Blanco," I said to help my friend. "All I heard Barry say was that he thought Amber looked *tarrific* today. He was just making a joke."

"*Tarrific*, huh?" Mr. Blanco rubbed his chin. "That's pretty clever of you, Barry."

"Uh, thanks, Mr. Blanco." Barry nodded awkwardly.

"But why don't you keep that cleverness to yourself, okay?" Mr. Blanco said sternly. "If you all give the same answers on this test, the state

4

education department will be sure to notice. That will reflect badly on Burt Itchupt Middle School. In other words, no more talking."

We all nodded silently.

Mr. Blanco walked away.

"You're dead meat, Andy," Barry muttered under his breath as soon as the principal was out of earshot.

"Why?" Andy asked. "Jake saved you, didn't he?"

"Doesn't matter," Barry grumbled ominously.

2

You had to feel sorry for Andy. Barry was a total sadist and a master at arm twists, foot crushers, skull noogies, shoulder tweaks, and every kind of wedgy imaginable. And it wasn't a question of fighting back, either. Not only was Barry the meanest fighter in the grade, but he was bigger and stronger than everyone else. Even though we were only in eighth grade, Barry already shaved and had hair on his chest. If you ask me, he didn't even belong in middle school. He should have been in high school.

Especially the High School for Criminally Insane Sadistic Dimwits.

"All right, everyone, pencils down and turn your tests over." Mr. Blanco's voice blared out of a microphone in the front of the cafetorium. "Please remain seated until I excuse you."

I turned over my test and glanced back at Barry, hoping that maybe he'd changed his mind about killing Andy. But Barry only glowered at Andy and bared his teeth in a nasty snarl.

Ms. Rogers, the nicest teacher ever born, came down our aisle and picked up our tests. She had wavy black hair and blue eyes and was always smiling. She was our homeroom and social studies teacher and was married to Mr. Dirksen, our science teacher. He was the inventor of the Dirksen Intelligence Transfer System, or DITS, which was supposed to transfer knowledge from one person to another. But he'd never gotten it to work correctly. So far the only thing it had ever done was make me and my friends switch bodies with various other people and animals.

"So, did you all exercise your right to freedom of expression?" she asked, fanning her face with some papers. It was Bill of Rights Month at Burp It Up Middle School. All month long our teachers were supposed to remind us about the first ten amendments to the United States Constitution.

"What does it matter, Ms. Rogers?" asked Josh. "These tests don't count toward our grades."

"That's true," Ms. Rogers replied. "But sometimes, if a student does very, very well, the state education department recommends skipping him ahead a grade."

"I don't think you'll have to worry about that happening to us," I said.

"Good." Ms. Rogers patted my shoulder. "Because I'd hate to lose my favorite troublemakers."

She continued down the aisle, collecting the tests. I glanced back at Barry again. He glared at Andy and cracked his knuckles. It looked like Ms. Rogers might lose one of her favorite troublemakers after all.

3

"All right, students," Mr. Blanco announced over the microphone after all the tests had been collected. "The school day is over. You are free to go home or to your regular after-school activities."

Andy stood up and bit his lip nervously. You had to feel bad for him. The only regular after-school activity that Barry Dunn ever participated in was called "Mashing Kids."

"See you around, Kent," Barry muttered ominously at Andy, then left the cafetorium ahead of us.

"Think he's going to wait for Andy out in the hall?" I asked.

"No way," said Josh. "Barry doesn't beat up kids in school anymore. That only gets him into trouble with Mr. Blanco. He'll wait somewhere off school property, then spring a surprise attack when Andy least expects it."

"Oh, great," Andy groaned woefully.

"Maybe you should sneak out through the gym, Andy," I suggested. "That way Barry won't see you."

"Forget it," Josh said. "You can't avoid him, Andy. You're a marked man. Sooner or later Barry's going to get you. You'll just have to take the bad with the good."

"*Good?*" Andy scowled. "I know what the bad part is. But what's good about it?"

"It'll be good when it's over," Josh said with a grin.

"That's easy for *you* to say, Josh," I said. "*You're* not the one who's going to have crushed toes. You're not the one who's going to have a bump on your head the size of Mount Everest after Barry gets finished noogying you. You're not the one who's going to be missing teeth, and have two black eyes, and a broken — "

"Stop it!" Andy cried.

I frowned. "What's with you?"

"Stop talking about what Barry's going to do to me," Andy pleaded. "You're totally wigging me out."

"Hey, guys, want to sign my petition?" Amanda Gluck came up carrying a clipboard with some sheets of paper on it. The right to petition was part of the freedom of speech, which was part of the Bill of Rights. Lately it seemed that every kid in school had a petition they wanted you to sign.

"What's it for?" I asked.

"A school dress code," answered Amanda. She was a brownnose, goody-two-shoes teacher's pet and the only girl in school who wore a dress every day.

"Why would we want a dress code?" Josh asked.

"Because then everyone will dress neatly," Amanda replied. "We won't have any slobs like you."

"Me? What's wrong with the way I'm dressed?" Josh asked. He was wearing baggy shorts and a black T-shirt with the sleeves torn off.

"No offense, Josh," said Amanda, "but you're dressed like a dirtbag."

"Oh, yeah?" Josh smiled. "Well, for your information, by dressing like this I'm exercising a right bestowed upon me by the United States Constitution."

"Freedom of expression?" Amanda guessed.

"Nope." Josh raised his sleeveless arms and flexed his muscles. "The right to bare arms."

"That's not what the Second Amendment means!" Amanda cried.

"It was a joke, Amanda," I said.

We left the cafetorium and walked to the school lobby. Andy stopped by the front doors and looked outside. "What if Barry's hiding somewhere, waiting to pounce?"

"You could accuse him of violating your constitutional right against cruel and unusual punishment," I suggested.

"Forget it," Andy griped sourly. "Barry doesn't know about the Bill of Rights. All he knows is the Bill of *Wrongs*."

"Hey, isn't that Jessica?" Josh pointed outside.

Down at the curb, my sister, Jessica, was sitting in the passenger seat of a green Jeep. I hadn't noticed her because she was wearing sunglasses. Her friend Cathy was in the driver's seat. She was wearing sunglasses, too.

"You're right," I said.

"This is your lucky day, Andy," said Josh. "Now that Jessica's here, we can get a ride home. Barry won't be able to get you."

"Maybe," Andy said cautiously. "But we still have to get from here to the car."

4

Deciding to run for it, we pushed open the school doors and dashed across the walk. Josh and I didn't actually have to run because of Barry, but we did it so Andy wouldn't feel alone.

"Okay!" I yelled as we piled into the back of the Jeep. "Let's go!"

Jessica slowly turned her head, lifted her sunglasses, and looked down her nose at us. "Go where?"

"Home! The mall! You name it!" Andy cried nervously. "Let's just get out of here!"

My sister gave her friend Cathy a look. Cathy had just gotten her license, and now she and my sister were The Coolest Girls Who Ever Lived. Their hair and clothes and makeup had to be cooler than everyone else's. And so did their attitudes. They'd rather die than look flustered by anything.

"Who said we were taking you anywhere?" Cathy asked Andy.

13

"What?!" Andy straightened up. "Weren't you waiting for Jake? Aren't you going to give Josh and me a ride?"

Jessica and Cathy looked at each other and laughed. Then Cathy put the Jeep in gear and pulled away from the curb.

"I guess they were just pulling your leg," I said to Andy.

Andy slumped down in the seat and nodded. He looked relieved. Meanwhile, Josh leaned forward and tapped Cathy on the shoulder.

"Cool car, Cathy," he said. "Think I could drive it?"

"No way," Cathy answered. "You're only in eighth grade."

"Yeah, but my dad taught me how to drive," Josh said. "We practice in the parking lot behind the mall. I'm a good driver."

"Get real, Josh," Cathy said.

She drove to Josh's house and parked in the shade under a tree.

Josh looked out the car window and groaned. "Oh, no, I forgot to cut the grass."

Cathy pointed at the thermometer in the Jeep. "What fun, Josh," she said with a chuckle. "It's only ninety degrees . . . in the shade."

"You're just a laugh and a half, Cathy," Josh grumbled, then turned to Andy and me. "Either of you guys feel like cutting my lawn? I'll be your best friend for life."

"Is that a promise or a threat?" I asked.

"I'll even pay you out of my own pocket," Josh promised. "Even though my dad makes me cut it for free."

"How much?" Andy asked.

"Five bucks," said Josh.

Andy and I peered out the window. Josh's house didn't have much of a lawn in the front, but there was an awful lot in the back.

We shook our heads.

"How about ten bucks?" Josh begged desperately.

Andy raised an interested eyebrow. "Just to cut it?"

"You have to pick up the cuttings and trim the edges, too," Josh added.

"Forget it." Andy shook his head.

"Some friends you guys are," Josh muttered and got out of the Jeep.

Cathy started to drive toward Andy's house.

"Don't go to my house!" Andy suddenly cried.

Jessica turned and gave him a puzzled look. "Why not?"

"I . . . er, I have to go to *your* house," he stammered.

"Why?" Jessica asked.

Andy didn't answer, so my sister turned her curious gaze on me. I knew Andy didn't want to admit to her that he was afraid to go home because Barry might be waiting for him.

"We have to go over some homework," I said, giving Andy a wink.

Cathy pulled the Jeep into our driveway. Jessica and I got out, but Andy stayed in the backseat and looked around nervously.

"I thought you were coming," Jessica said.

"In a second," Andy answered.

"Come on, Andy," I said impatiently. "Now you're being dumb. Barry can't be hiding in the bushes. He doesn't even know you're here."

"Who doesn't know Andy's here?" Jessica asked.

"No one." Andy hopped out of the Jeep and hurried toward the front door. I let him into the house. Jessica, being one of The Coolest Girls Who Ever Lived, took her time coming up the front walk. As soon as she was inside, Andy slammed the door behind her and bolted it.

"What's going on?" Jessica asked.

"Nothing," Andy replied.

We went into the kitchen. Andy quickly pulled the shades closed on the windows.

My sister gave me a puzzled look. "Would someone please tell me why Andy's acting like a team of hit men are looking for him?"

Andy and I shared a glance.

"You might as well tell her," I said.

"Barry Dunn," Andy admitted.

Briiinnnggg! The phone rang. Jessica reached to answer it.

"Wait!" Andy cried.

She stopped. "Now what?"

"It might be him," Andy said fearfully. "You can't tell him I'm here. Tell him I'm at the martial arts center learning karate. Better yet, tell him I'm at the target range, practicing with my new machine gun."

Jessica rolled her eyes to let Andy know she thought he was being a jerk. She answered the phone: "Hello? Yes, Andy's here. You want to speak to him? Just a minute."

My sister put her hand over the receiver and held it toward Andy. "It's for you."

Andy turned pale. "Who is it?"

Jessica smiled. "Barry Dunn."

5

Andy's mouth fell open. "Why'd you tell him I was here?" he whimpered.

"Sorry." Jessica shrugged. "Guess I forgot." She held the receiver toward him. "You'd better take this before he gets *really* mad."

With trembling hands Andy took the receiver. "H-hello? Who? Wait, this doesn't sound like Barry. . . . What?!" Andy stared at Jessica, who grinned back. "You tricked me!"

Andy spoke into the phone again. "No, not you, Josh. Jessica said it was Barry on the phone."

Jessica and I could hear Josh laugh on the other end of the line.

"You just love it, don't you?" Andy grumbled sourly into the phone. "What? No, I can't take a joke, okay? Not when it might mean a Mega-Wedgy or Total Noogification. So why'd you call? Oh, okay. Uh-huh. Uh-huh. What? Very funny, jerkface."

Andy hung up the phone.

"What'd he say?" I asked.

"His parents are going away tomorrow," Andy reported. "The neighbors are going to look in on him, but he'll be alone a lot. He says we should get ready to party . . . *if* Barry doesn't get me first."

"He really knows how to make a guy feel good," I observed.

"I can't believe you're worried about noogies and wedgies," my sister said. "That's nothing compared to what goes on in high school."

"Like what?" Andy asked.

"Well, did you know that Cathy's boyfriend's best friend is Sharkbait McGuire?" Jessica asked.

"What kind of name is that?" I asked.

"It's his nickname," Jessica said.

"How'd he get it?" asked Andy.

"All I know is that he has a boat and he likes to fish for sharks," Jessica said. "There was some guy named Freddy who Sharkbait didn't like, so he took him fishing. When Sharkbait came back, he'd caught a five-hundred-pound man-eating tiger shark."

"So?" I said.

"No one ever saw Freddy again," Jessica said.

"No way," I scoffed. "I don't believe that."

"I swear it's true," said my sister. "You can ask anyone."

Andy and I stared at each other. Andy swallowed. "No wonder they call him 'Sharkbait.' Is he really Cathy's boyfriend's best friend?"

Jessica nodded.

For the first time that day I saw a smile creep across Andy's lips. Meanwhile Jessica said she was going to her room to change clothes.

"What are you smiling about?" I asked Andy when my sister had left.

"Sharkbait McGuire," Andy answered. "I think I just found the perfect anti–Barry Dunn weapon."

6

The next morning, my friends and I trudged to school in the heat.

"I can't believe my mother," Josh griped. "She and my dad go away for the week and does she leave me lunch money? No. Instead, she leaves half a million peanut-butter-and-jelly sandwiches in the refrigerator."

"So what's the big deal?" Andy asked.

"The big deal is maybe I'd like to eat something else once in a while," Josh complained. "And not only that. You know what happens to peanut butter and jelly on hot days like this? It gets totally runny and seeps into the bread and becomes a big glob of disgusting mush."

"Well, to quote *you*, Josh," Andy said with a wink, "I guess you'll just have to take the bad with the good. It may be mush, but at least it's lunch."

"Why are you in such a good mood?" Josh asked him.

"Why shouldn't I be?" Andy asked back.

"Maybe because Barry Dunn has you marked for destruction."

Andy just smiled. "Barry Dunn is an overgrown troll with the brains of a speed bump."

"What'd you say?" a voice suddenly growled behind us.

My friends and I froze. I felt the hair on the back of my neck stand up. Turning slowly, we found Barry standing behind us with a lethal sneer on his face. He was pushing his sleeves up his arms and balling his hands into fists. "The brains of a speed bump, huh?" he snarled at Andy. "When I get finished with you, you won't have no brains left at all."

"Run, Andy!" I cried.

But even though he was trembling, Andy didn't budge.

Barry looked surprised. "How come you're not running away, wimp?"

"Because y-you're not going to t-touch me," Andy stammered.

The lines between Barry's eyes deepened. "Why not?"

"B-because I'll send Sh-Sharkbait McGuire after you."

"Who?" Barry asked.

"The m-meanest, n-nastiest guy in Jeffersonville," Andy said.

"Why do they call him Sharkbait?" Barry asked.

Andy told him the story of how Sharkbait McGuire took a guy he didn't like fishing. And how he came back with a tiger shark but no guy.

"Oh, yeah?" Barry smirked. "And what makes you think he'd protect a twirp like you?"

"Because he's the best friend of the boyfriend of Jake's sister's best friend," Andy said.

Barry scowled. "The boyfriend of the best friend of Jake's sister's best friend?"

"No, the best friend of the boyfriend of my sister's best friend," I corrected him.

"That's what I said," said Barry.

"No," I said. "You said he was the boyfriend of the best friend of my sister's best friend. But he's really the best friend of the boyfriend of my sister's best friend."

"Wait a minute," Josh interrupted us. "What difference does it make?"

Barry suddenly grinned and grabbed Andy by the shirt collar. "It sure don't make no difference to me."

7

When we got to school a little while later, Andy was limping. He had a big bump on his head, and one of his eyes was swollen and black-and-blue. Barry had worked him over pretty good.

"You had to open your big mouth and ask what difference it made," he grumbled bitterly at Josh.

"Believe me, Andy, after you made that speed bump crack Barry was going to beat you up no matter what," Josh replied with a shrug. He turned toward the library. "I have to drop off some books. See you guys at lunch."

Andy and I waved good-bye and went into homeroom.

"Want me to ask Jessica to ask Cathy if her boyfriend can get Sharkbait McGuire to beat up Barry?" I asked as we took our seats.

"What's the point?" Andy replied miserably. "What if Barry was right? I don't know Sharkbait McGuire. Why would he do anything for me?"

The classroom door opened and Ollie Hawkins came in. He was a small kid with blond hair and glasses who had recently moved to Jeffersonville from Ohio.

"Hey, Ollie," I said. "You're in the wrong homeroom."

"I want you guys to sign my petition," Ollie replied, holding up a sheet of paper filled with signatures.

"What's it for?" I asked.

"Sports teams for small guys like me," Ollie answered. "There are a lot of us smaller guys who really like to play basketball and football, but we always get cut from teams because we're not big enough. So we want teams of our own to play on."

"Like a shrimp league?" Andy asked.

"Exactly," said Ollie.

It sounded reasonable and most of the kids in our homeroom agreed to sign the petition. Then Ms. Rogers came in and Ollie asked her to sign it, too.

"This is great," Ollie said after our teacher signed it. "Almost half the kids in school have put their names on it, and a lot of the teachers, too. I can't wait to bring it to Principal Blanco."

Ms. Rogers smiled crookedly as if she knew something Ollie didn't know. "I'll be interested in how he responds, Ollie. Now you'd better get to your homeroom."

Ollie left and Ms. Rogers took attendance and

made some announcements. Homeroom always went pretty fast, and it wasn't long before the bell rang.

As Andy and I got up to leave, Ms. Rogers said, "Could you stay for a second, Andy?"

Andy and I stayed behind and waited until the rest of the class left.

When the room was empty, Ms. Rogers stepped close to Andy and studied his face. "Did someone hurt you?"

Andy and I shared a furtive glance. We both knew what would happen if Andy ratted on Barry. Barry would really kill him. Luckily Ms. Rogers was smart enough to know exactly what we were thinking.

"I promise I won't tell Principal Blanco," she said in a low voice. "It was Barry Dunn, right?"

"Can't the school do anything about him?" I asked.

"Did he do this to you on school grounds?" Ms. Rogers asked Andy.

Andy shook his head.

"He never does anything to kids on school grounds anymore," I said. "He waits to get you when you're not in school."

Ms. Rogers crossed her arms, leaned against her desk, and thought hard for a moment. Finally she shook her head. "If it's off school grounds there's nothing we can do," she said regretfully. "I'm sorry, boys."

8

My friends and I played punchball after lunch, but it was so hot that we came in after a while to get a drink. Andy and I were heading for the cafetorium when Josh said, "Not that way, guys."

We stopped. "Don't you want to get some water?"

"Sure, but the water in the cafetorium is always warm," Josh said. "Let's use the fountain outside the teachers' lounge. It's got the coldest water in the building."

We went down to the teachers' lounge. On the wall outside the lounge was a poster reminding teachers about the annual blood drive. The door to the lounge was slightly ajar and we could hear the teachers inside talking.

"I'm sorry, Kim, but it's just not realistic to have teams for small players," a man's voice said while we took drinks from the fountain in the hall.

"That sounds like Principal Blanco," Josh whispered to me. "And isn't Ms. Rogers's first name Kim?"

I nodded. Meanwhile in the teachers' lounge, Ms. Rogers said, "I don't see why not."

"Because small players will never have a chance to go on to the pros," Principal Blanco explained.

"That's not the point," Ms. Rogers protested. "Realistically speaking, the chance of *any* student from this school becoming a professional athlete is practically zero."

"You always take the side of the underdog," Principal Blanco shot back accusingly. "I don't have time to argue about this, Kim. If you insist on discussing it further, you can come to my office."

"You're always busy when I come to your office," Ms. Rogers answered.

"From now on I'm going to have an open-door policy," Principal Blanco announced. "Come to my office any time and I'll drop whatever I'm doing and speak to you."

Suddenly the door to the teachers' lounge swung open and Principal Blanco stepped out. He frowned when he saw us. "What are you boys doing out here?"

"Uh, just getting a drink," I said as my friends and I backed away.

"You're supposed to use the fountain in the cafetorium," our principal said.

"But that water's never cold," Josh complained.

"This fountain is off-limits to students," Principal Blanco replied.

"What if we start a petition?" I asked.

"I've had it up to *here* with those darn petitions," Principal Blanco answered angrily. "Get to your next class!"

Our next class was science, so we started toward the science wing.

"Sounds like Blanco and Ms. Rogers were arguing over Ollie's idea for the shrimp league," Josh said.

"I wish they'd argue over how to get rid of Barry instead," Andy muttered.

"Funny you should say that," I answered in a low voice. Down the hall Barry was hanging around with some of his friends.

Andy stopped. "Maybe we should go another way."

"But this is the only way to get to science," I said.

By now Barry had noticed us. He grinned menacingly at Andy and smacked his fist into his hand. "How you feeling, Andy?"

"Looks like Kent got some dents," one of his friends chuckled.

"Still think I'm as dumb as a speed bump?" Barry asked as my friends and I made a wide circle around him.

"Oh, no," replied Andy. "You're so smart you

stared at a container of orange juice because it said 'concentrate.' "

"You think I don't get that?" Barry asked.

"I don't get it," one of his friends said.

While Barry tried to explain it, my friends and I scrambled to the safety of the science wing.

"I still say Principal Blanco should expel Barry," Andy grumbled.

"You heard Ms. Rogers this morning," I said. "He can't."

"I would if I was principal," said Josh.

"How?" Andy asked.

"Easy," Josh said. "I'd make a new rule. Something Barry was bound to break. And as soon as he did, I'd expel him."

Andy and I stopped and stared at him. We were in the science wing, standing in the hall outside Mr. Dirksen's lab. *Inside* Mr. Dirksen's lab was the DITS.

"That easy, huh?" Andy smiled.

"If you were principal," I said.

Josh blinked and stepped back. "Hey, wait! No way! I wasn't serious! Forget it, Andy!"

9

The next day after school, Andy and I met in Mr. Dirksen's science lab.

"Did you bring the stuff?" he asked.

"Sure did." I opened my backpack and pulled out a roll of masking tape, a pencil flashlight, and the mini-DITS, a miniature version of the Dirksen Intelligence Transfer System. Mr. Dirksen had asked me to keep it for the summer while he and Ms. Rogers went on a dangerous expedition to the Amazon. Ms. Rogers had come back, but Mr. Dirksen was staying in Brazil on a sabbatical.

"I don't get it, Andy," I said. "Why do we need the mini-DITS if you want to use the regular DITS?"

"As a backup," Andy replied, taking a rubber doorstop and a glow-in-the-dark yo-yo out of his backpack.

"What's with the yo-yo?" I asked.

"It was the only thing I could find that glows,"

he said. "We have to hurry. Turn off the lights and put a lot of tape over the light switch."

"Right." I started taping the light switch. "So, how many kids did you get to sign your petition?"

That morning Andy had circulated a secret petition for kids who would agree to cut Josh's lawn if we could get Barry Dunn kicked out of school for good.

"I stopped at forty," Andy answered. "There were more kids who wanted to sign up, but Josh doesn't have *that* much lawn."

"You didn't tell them our plan, did you?" I asked.

"No way," Andy promised. "Besides, they don't care *how* we get rid of Barry as long as we do it. Given the choice between cutting lawns and getting smeared by Barry, you'd do the same thing."

"If this plan doesn't work, we're going to get in more trouble than we've ever been in our entire lives," I warned him.

"Tell me about it," Andy answered with a nod.

The lab door opened and Josh came in with Amber Sweeny. Amber always gave me goose bumps with her piercing green eyes. Every guy in the eighth grade had a crush on her, especially Andy.

Andy gave Josh a surprised, questioning look. "What's going on?"

"I want you to swear before a witness," Josh

explained. "Raise your left hand and take off your shoes and socks."

"Why?" Andy asked.

"So I know you're not crossing your toes."

"I swear I won't cross my toes," Andy promised, holding up his left hand.

"Pinkie swear." Josh and Andy hooked pinkies.

"Repeat after me," Josh said. "I, Andy Kent."

"I, Andy Kent."

"Do solemnly swear to make sure Josh Hopka's lawn is cut for the next two years."

"Do solemnly swear to make sure Josh Hopka's lawn is cut for the next two years," Andy repeated.

"Including picking up the cuttings and trimming the edges."

"Including picking up the cuttings and trimming the edges," Andy repeated.

"As well as weeding the flower beds and watering when necessary."

"No way!" Andy pulled his pinkie away. "That wasn't part of the deal we made yesterday."

"I changed my mind," Josh said.

"Not a chance, Josh," Andy countered. "We made a deal. You can't add to it now."

Josh shrugged. "It was worth a try." He turned to Amber. "You saw Andy pinkie swear, right?"

Amber nodded.

"And no fingers, toes, or other limbs were crossed, correct?" Josh asked.

"Correct," Amber replied.

Josh turned to Andy. "Let this be permanently burned into your brain, Andy. If you don't keep your part of the deal you will be forever haunted by the knowledge that Amber Sweeny will think of you as a no-good weasel and pinkie-swear breaker."

"What's your half of the deal?" Amber asked Josh.

"Top secret," Josh replied. "You can go now."

Amber turned to Andy. "I don't know what's going on, Andy, but I hope you're getting something good out of this, too."

Andy's face turned red. "Better believe it."

As soon as Amber left the lab, Andy glared daggers at Josh. "You had to bring *her* into it."

"Now I know you'll keep your half of the deal," Josh replied with a knowing smile.

"So how are we going to get Principal Blanco in here to switch bodies with Josh?" I asked.

"Easy." Andy picked up the classroom wall phone near the door and spoke into it: "Attention, main office! There's a problem in Mr. Dirksen's lab. Please send Principal Blanco immediately."

Then he hung up.

"Now what?" I asked.

Andy nodded at the DITS. It was a large computer terminal with chairs on either side of it. Andy put the glow-in-the-dark yo-yo on one chair.

"Josh, you sit in the other chair while Jake and I pull the shades."

The shades in the lab were specially made to block all outside light so that Mr. Dirksen could darken the room for science experiments. There was even a small shade for the door window.

"I can't see my hand in front of my face," I said once all the shades were down. Except for the dull glow of the plastic yo-yo, it was pitch-black in the lab.

"Are you sitting in the chair, Josh?" Andy asked in the dark.

"Yes," came the answer.

"Hide, Jake," Andy said. "As soon as Mr. Blanco comes in, close the door behind him and jam in the doorstop so he can't get out."

I hid behind the door. In the meantime, Andy took out the penlight and made his way over to the DITS. He flicked on the power switch and put his finger on the red button. Then he turned off the penlight.

Once again the room became pitch-black.

"Okay, guys," Andy whispered in the dark. "Now we keep our fingers crossed and wait."

We didn't have to wait long. Soon we heard the hurried slap of shoe leather coming down the hall. The doorknob turned and the door swung open. Principal Blanco stood in the doorway.

"Did someone say there was an emergency?"

he asked, trying to peer into the dark lab. "Is anyone here?"

No one said a word. Principal Blanco took a tentative step into the classroom and reached for the light switch.

Bang! I slammed the door behind him and jammed in the rubber doorstop.

"What the . . . ?" Principal Blanco spun around in the darkness and pulled on the doorknob. Thanks to the doorstop, the door wouldn't open.

"All right," Principal Blanco said angrily. "What kind of game is this? Whoever's behind this is going to regret it."

I prayed Andy's plan would work. For a moment I heard nothing. Then footsteps toward the DITS. In the darkness I could just make out the vague shape of Principal Blanco as he leaned over the chair to pick up the glow-in-the-dark yo-yo.

Then Andy must've pushed the button, because the next thing I heard was a loud *Whump!*

10

"What in the world?" someone gasped in the dark. It was Josh's voice, but those weren't Josh's words.

"This is totally weird." That was Principal Blanco's voice but definitely not his words, either.

Andy's plan had worked!

"Jake?" Andy called in the dark.

"Yeah?"

"Untape the light switch and turn on the lights."

"Tape on the light switch?" Josh's voice barked angrily in the dark. "What is going on?"

"Chill out, Mr. Blanco," Andy answered.

"Andy Kent?" Josh's voice was filled with surprise. "Was that you? Kent, if this is one of your tricks you are going to be one very sorry young — "

The lights went on. It took a moment for everyone's eyes to adjust. Once they did, I saw my friend Josh standing next to one of the DITS chairs. His mouth had fallen open and he was staring at Principal Blanco, who was standing next to the other DITS chair. The principal was looking down at the backs of his hands.

"Whoa, hairy hands!" The principal's mouth formed the words, but we knew it was Josh who had spoken.

"I don't understand," said our friend Josh, whose body was now inhabited by Principal Blanco. The principal looked down at himself in Josh's body. He stared at Josh's hands and the sleeveless T-shirt and baggy shorts he was wearing.

"This isn't my body," said Blanco in Josh's body.

"It is now," said Andy.

Blanco in Josh's body stared at him. "What's going on, Kent? What did you do to us?"

"I switched you with Josh," Andy explained. "Now he has your body and you have his."

Once again Principal Blanco stared down at his new teenage body. "I'm not going to bother asking how you did this, Kent. It obviously has something to do with Dirksen's machine. But I order you to switch us back immediately."

"Sure," Andy replied. "On one condition. You have to expel Barry Dunn from school forever."

"I . . . I can't do that," stammered Blanco in Josh's body.

"Sure you can," Andy said. "You're the number

one guy. The big cheese. The absolute commander and chief of Burp It Up Middle School."

Principal Blanco shook Josh's head. "I still can't expel a student for no reason."

"I'll give you a reason," I said. "Barry beats up everyone."

"But he never does it on school grounds," explained Blanco in Josh's body. "So I have no authority."

"Well, if you won't get rid of Barry, *he* will." Andy pointed at Josh in the principal's body. Josh waved Blanco's hand.

With a stunned expression on his face, Blanco in Josh's body turned to Josh in his. "So that's what this is all about! Well, I'm sorry, but it won't work, Josh. Just because you have my body doesn't mean you can expel Dunn."

"Wrong!" cackled Josh in the principal's body.

"Who are you to tell me I'm wrong?" demanded Blanco in Josh's body.

"I'm *you*," replied Josh with a smile. "And now that I'm the big kahuna around here, I can do anything I want."

11

We waited to see how Principal Blanco in Josh's body would react. Meanwhile, Josh in Blanco's body stuck his hands into the principal's suit pockets.

"Wow, I never wore a suit before," he said. "What do you need all these pockets for?"

"What do you think you're doing?" Blanco in Josh's body demanded.

"I'm going through your pockets," Josh replied.

"I order you to stop!" Blanco demanded.

"With all due respect, *sir*," replied Josh in the principal's body, "I think you better get used to the fact that you're not Principal Blanco anymore. *I am*. You're an eighth grader named Josh Hopka. You don't order *me* around. *I* order *you* around, understand?"

As if he were suddenly dizzy, Blanco pressed Josh's hand against his forehead. "I can't believe this is happening!"

Meanwhile, Josh in Blanco pulled a thick ring of

keys out of the principal's suit pocket. "Whoa! Now I can get into all kinds of cool places."

"Those aren't yours!" Blanco in Josh cried.

"Wanna bet?" Josh in the principal's body smiled as he went through the rings. "Hey, what's this?"

Attached to the key ring was a small tube the size of a lipstick, but it had little snippers on the end.

"It's nothing," said Blanco in Josh's body. "Forget about it."

Josh in the principal's body turned to Andy and me. "What do you think, guys? Should we forget about it?"

Andy and I shook our heads. We were genuinely curious.

Josh in the principal's body grinned at Blanco in Josh. "I suggest you tell us what this is . . . or I just might declare tomorrow a snow day."

"But it went over ninety today!" argued Blanco in Josh's body. "We're in the middle of a heat wave!"

Josh in the principal's body walked over to the wall phone and started to pick it up. "One call does it all."

"Okay, okay, I'll tell you." Blanco in Josh sighed. "It's a nose hair clipper."

"A *what*?" I asked.

"When you get older," Blanco in Josh explained, "you start to grow hair out of your ears and nostrils. If you want to be well groomed, you must attend to those places."

"Nostril hairs, huh?" Josh tilted Blanco's head back. "Hey, Andy, take a look and tell me if the principal's nostril hairs need attention."

"Forget it." Andy shook his head. "I'm not looking up your nose."

"Yes, you will, slave!" Josh in Blanco bellowed. "As the absolute commander in chief of this school, I *order* you to inspect my nose immediately!"

"Oh, okay." Andy went over and looked up the principal's nostrils. "I'd say he's been doing a pretty good job up there."

"How about the ears?" Josh lowered the principal's head so that Andy could inspect the ears.

"Naw, he's not doing too good in the ear department," Andy said. "He's got some major curly ones in there that should have been trimmed back a long time ago. And talk about earwax!"

"This is ridiculous!" sputtered Blanco in Josh's body. "I can't believe a bunch of teenage nitwits are criticizing my personal grooming habits. I can't believe one of them *has my body!*"

"Better get used to it," Andy advised.

Blanco in Josh glared at him. "Well, it's not as if the only thing I have to do in life is trim ear hairs. I've got a school to run."

"Not anymore," said Josh in the principal's

body. He handed the clippers to Andy. "Fix the ears."

"My pleasure." Andy trimmed the hairs in and around the principal's ears. "There you go."

"Thank you, slave," said Josh in the principal's body. "Now what about the earwax?"

Andy turned to Blanco in Josh and held up the ear hair clipper. "Does this thing have an earwax scoop or something?"

"Not that I know of," huffed Blanco in Josh.

"*Tsk, tsk.*" Josh in Blanco's body turned to the principal in his. "You really ought to pay more attention to personal hygiene. Long ear hairs and waxy ears can reflect badly on a school's image."

"*That's it!*" Andy suddenly cried. "I just figured out how we can get Barry expelled!"

12

Since Josh now had Principal Blanco's body, as well as his wallet and keys, it was easy for him to figure out where the principal lived. The principal in Josh's body nearly freaked out when Josh got into his car, but Josh assured him that he knew how to drive and that he wouldn't leave the lights on in Blanco's house when he left for school the next morning.

Meanwhile, Andy and I dropped Blanco in Josh's body off at Josh's house and explained that his parents were away and that there were plenty of peanut-butter-and-jelly sandwiches in the refrigerator if he got hungry.

The next morning, Andy and I stopped at Josh's house to pick up the principal in our friend's body. Even though it was still early, the sun felt hot. It was shaping up to be another scalding day, but Blanco in Josh came out of the house wearing creased brown slacks and a pressed blue long-sleeved shirt. His shoulders were stooped and he was hanging his head.

"Hey, Principal Blanco," Andy said. "As one horse said to another, why the long face?"

"I called everyone I knew last night," moped Blanco in Josh's body. "I tried to explain that I'd been tricked into switching bodies with an irresponsible middle schooler, but not a single person believed me. I guess it was stupid of me to think they might."

"Hey, look at the bright side," I said. "You don't have to work today. You can fool around as much as you want."

Blanco in Josh's body stiffened. "No, I can't. I have to go to school."

"That's what I meant." I winked.

"You mean, now that I'm in Josh's body, I can fool around as much as I want *in school*?" Blanco in Josh asked.

"Why not?" Andy smiled. "That's what we do!"

Blanco shook Josh's head stubbornly. "Never! That's just what you're hoping for, isn't it? You'd love to see me, your principal, cut up and get into trouble. Well, forget it. I don't care whose body I'm in. As long as I'm a student, I intend to set an example of serious studiousness."

"Have it your way," I said with a shrug.

We walked to school and had just gotten into homeroom when Principal Blanco's voice crackled over the loudspeaker. "Attention, all teachers, students, and other genetic accidents, this is Mr. Hop . . . er, I mean, Mr. Blanco speaking. You will all proceed immediately to the cafetorium for an emergency assembly."

"An emergency assembly?" Amber Sweeny repeated. "I've never heard of that."

"Neither have I," said Ms. Rogers. "Okay, class, let's go see what it's all about."

As Andy and I got up, we shared a secret smile. We already knew what it was all about.

Out in the hall, we met up with Blanco in Josh's body. He was the only kid in the hall wearing long pants and a long-sleeved shirt.

"I assume you two know what this is about," he muttered.

"Sure do," Andy said gleefully. "It's about getting rid of one overgrown muscle-brained troll with the mental capacity of a tree stump."

Slap! Without warning, a hand clamped down on Andy's shoulder and spun him around.

The next thing we knew, Andy was face-to-face with Barry Dunn. And Barry looked angry!

13

A nasty snarl slithered across Barry's lips. "Still talking trash about me, huh, Kent?"

"Uh . . . uh . . ." Andy opened his mouth but couldn't get any words out.

Wham! Barry slammed him against the lockers. "I thought you learned your lesson."

"I did!" Andy squirmed. "Really, Barry! You have to believe me! It was a good lesson! One of the best I've ever learned!"

"How many times do I have to tell you that I'm smarter than I look?" Barry growled.

"Let go of him, Dunn," ordered Principal Blanco in Josh's body with his arms crossed.

Barry blinked at Blanco in Josh as if he couldn't believe what he'd just heard. "What did you say?"

"I said, unhand that student," Blanco in our friend's body repeated sternly.

Barry loosened his grip on Andy. With a look of pure astonishment on his face, he turned to Josh.

"That's much better, Dunn." Blanco in Josh's

body nodded approvingly. "And don't let me see any more roughhousing in these halls, understand?"

Barry stepped toward Josh and started to crack his knuckles. "You talkin' to me, Hopka?"

"Hopka?" Josh's mouth fell open, as if Blanco had just remembered whose body he was in. "Oh! Ha-ha-Hopka," he stammered.

"D-d-*dead* Ha-ha-Hopka," Barry growled, holding up a fist under Josh's trembling nose.

"That's enough," Ms. Rogers suddenly interrupted. She was standing behind us, looking angry. "Barry, if I catch you menacing students again, I'll send you straight to Principal Blanco's office."

Barry gave Blanco in Josh a withering look and moved his lips silently as if to say, "I'll get you after school."

"Move it, Barry," Ms. Rogers commanded.

Muttering to himself, Barry joined the crowd headed for the cafetorium. Ms. Rogers walked with my friends and me.

"I'm sorry, boys," she apologized. "I know you wish I'd do more than just threaten Barry. But it wouldn't be fair. I can't treat him differently than any other student."

"I'm afraid I have to agree with you, Kim," said Blanco in Josh's body.

Ms. Rogers frowned. "Excuse me, Josh, but did you just call me Kim?"

"Oh, uh, I meant, Ms. Rogers," Blanco in Josh's body quickly said.

The cafetorium was crowded with kids and teachers. A lot of them were staring at the stage with puzzled expressions on their faces.

"What in the world?" Ms. Rogers asked out loud.

Josh in Principal Blanco's body was standing on the stage. Only, he wasn't *dressed* like the principal. Instead of the usual dark suit, he was wearing baggy shorts and a T-shirt with the sleeves torn off. On his right biceps was a tattoo of a big red heart with an arrow through it. On his left biceps was a tattoo of a black spiderweb.

"Looks like Josh was busy last night," Andy quipped as we sat down.

"What did you say?" Ms. Rogers asked.

"Oh, uh, nothing, Ms. Rogers," Andy quickly replied.

Meanwhile Blanco in Josh's body slumped down next to us. "Tattoos!" he moaned despairingly. "I'll kill him. I swear, I'm going to tear him limb from limb."

"Who?" Ms. Rogers asked with a frown.

Blanco in Josh straightened up in surprise. "Oh, uh, no one, Kim."

Ms. Rogers scowled. "Did you just call me Kim again?"

Blanco bit Josh's lip nervously. "Uh . . ."

Click! Click! Click! Up on the stage, Josh in

the principal's body flicked the microphone with his fingernail. "Okay, meat brains, listen up! It's time we made some changes in the way this school is run."

"Oh, no!" Blanco in Josh's body buried his face in his hands. Ms. Rogers gave him a puzzled look.

"Doctors at the Nintendo Institute of Higher Education," Josh in the principal's body went on, "have discovered a direct relationship between personal grooming and academic performance. They have specifically isolated untrimmed ear and nostril hair as the major contributors to poor grades and misbehavior in school. Therefore, starting tomorrow morning, I will be conducting random inspections of all noses and ears. Any student caught with untrimmed ear and nostril hair will be immediately expelled. That is all. You may now proceed to your first period class."

Josh in the principal's body walked off the stage. Loud bewildered murmurs began to ripple through the students and teachers in the cafetorium.

"He can't be serious!"

"It's not April Fools' Day, is it?"

"That's the strangest thing I've ever heard!"

"How do you trim nostril hairs, anyway?"

I looked over at Blanco in Josh's body. He was facedown on the table with his head buried in his arms.

"Josh, are you okay?" Ms. Rogers asked.

Blanco shook our friend's head without looking up. "I'm finished! Ruined! My career is going down the drain!"

"What career?" Ms. Rogers asked. "What are you talking about? You're a student."

"Maybe he's really fond of his nostril hairs," Andy guessed.

"Well, I think it's the most ridiculous thing I've ever heard," Ms. Rogers said. "The Nintendo Institute of Higher Education. What nonsense! As soon as I have a free moment today I'm going to give Principal Blanco a piece of my mind."

Blanco raised Josh's head from the table. "It won't do any good."

"Why not?" Ms. Rogers asked.

I could tell from the look on his face that Blanco in Josh had decided to tell Ms. Rogers the truth.

He started to speak. "Because the person you think is Principal Blanco is really — "

"Not himself today," I quickly blurted before he could finish.

Blanco in Josh's body frowned. "That's not what I was going to say."

"What were you going to say?" Ms. Rogers asked.

Before Blanco in Josh's body could answer, the loudspeaker crackled overhead: "Jake Sherman, Andy Kent, and Josh Hopka. Please come to the main office. Principal Blanco wants to see you immediately."

51

14

The faint lines across Ms. Rogers's forehead deepened. "Now what?"

Andy tilted his head back and pointed at his nostrils. "Take a look, Jake. Think I'm in trouble?"

"I'm not interested in looking up your nose," I replied.

"I thought Principal Blanco said the inspections won't begin until tomorrow," said Ms. Rogers.

"Come with me, you two," Blanco in Josh's body said sullenly. "I'll bet I know *exactly* why he wants to see us."

"Why, Josh?" asked Ms. Rogers.

Blanco in Josh's body gazed sadly at her. For a second I feared that he might try to tell her the truth again. But then he sighed and shrugged. "Forget it, Kim, you'd never believe me."

"I really don't think you should be addressing me by my first name," Ms. Rogers said disapprovingly.

"Yeah, Josh," Andy said. "Have you forgotten who you are? You're just a slimy little eighth grader like the rest of us. We never address teachers by their first names, do we, Jake?"

"Never," I said.

Blanco in Josh's body glared at me with so much fury that I felt a chill run down my arms.

"But you are right about one thing, Josh," I said as I grabbed his sleeve and tugged him away from Ms. Rogers. "We definitely better go see what Principal Blanco wants."

Andy and I led Blanco in our friend's body out of the cafetorium and down the hall toward the main office.

"So what are you going to do about Barry?" Andy asked.

"Why should I do anything about him?" replied Blanco in Josh.

"Didn't you read his lips before?" Andy asked. "He said he was going to get you after school."

"I'm sure that was just an idle threat," Blanco in Josh replied.

"I wouldn't be so sure if I were you," warned Andy.

"I'll tell you what else I'm sure of, boys," said Blanco in Josh as we walked. "I swore I'd never expel a student from this school, but I've changed my mind."

"You mean, you'll expel Barry after all?" Andy asked hopefully.

"No." Blanco shook Josh's head. "But as soon as I get back into my own body, I'm definitely going to expel *you*!"

Andy and I shared a nervous look as we pushed open the door to the main office. Inside, everything looked pretty normal. White-haired Mrs. Hub was sitting at her desk as usual, and the other office secretaries were answering phones and typing on computers. On the wall was another one of those blood drive posters.

The only strange thing was the loud thumping music coming from behind the closed door to the principal's office. Mrs. Hub gave us a curious look.

"We're here to see Principal Blanco," I said.

Mrs. Hub pulled a wad of tissue out of each ear. "What did you say?"

"I said, we're here to see the principal!" I yelled.

"Go on in!" Mrs. Hub yelled back and stuffed the tissues back into her ears.

Andy pushed open Blanco's door and we went in. Inside, Josh in the principal's body was sitting with his feet up on Blanco's big wooden desk. On his lap was a keyboard, and he was typing on the principal's computer. A small boom box on the shelf behind the desk was blasting music at full volume.

"Get those feet off my desk!" Blanco in Josh's body shouted.

Josh in the principal's body didn't even look up from the computer.

Blanco in Josh's body reached over the desk and turned down the music. "I said, get your feet off my desk!"

Josh in the principal's body didn't budge. "Where'd you find those brown slacks? Why'd you have to dress like such a dork?"

Blanco in Josh straightened his sleeves. "I have news for you, Hopka. This is the best you've looked in years."

"What's with the music, Josh?" I asked.

"I'm thinking of playing it over the PA system tomorrow," Josh in the principal's body replied. "There'll be music in the classrooms all day. What do you think?"

"That's absurd," answered Blanco in our friend's body.

Josh in the principal's body ignored him and pointed at the computer screen. "Where do you get off paying Mr. Braun more than Ms. Rogers? Mr. Braun is a gym teacher. All he does is make us play games. At least Ms. Rogers *teaches* us something."

"How did you get into payroll?" Blanco in Josh gasped. "You need the password."

"You mean, 'dark suit'?" replied Josh in the principal.

Blanco in Josh sat down hard. "How in the world . . . ?"

"It was taped to your computer at home," Josh in the principal explained. "So what about Mr. Braun and Ms. Rogers?"

"It's done by seniority," Blanco in Josh's body explained. "Mr. Braun has been here longer so he makes more."

Josh in the principal's body turned to Andy and me. "Bet you didn't know this school spends four times more on sports than on books."

"Sounds right to me," Andy replied.

Josh rolled Blanco's eyes. "Of course you'd say that, Andy. What was I thinking?"

"Maybe you could tell us what you were thinking when you put on those ridiculous clothes this morning." Blanco in our friend's body was really steaming. "And I assume those tattoos are the wash-off variety."

"Nope, I had 'em done last night at the mall." Josh in Blanco's body reached into his pocket and pulled out a gold Visa card. "Visa, it's *everywhere* you want to be."

"I don't believe this!" Blanco in Josh slumped down in his seat and pressed his hands against his face.

On the other side of the desk, Josh in Blanco's body ran his finger down a column of numbers on the computer screen. "What's with this hefty number for teacher travel and enrichment?"

"We help pay for them to go to conferences so

they can learn to be better teachers," Blanco in Josh explained.

"What about the enrichment part?" Andy huffed. "Since when is it the school's job to make teachers rich?"

Blanco in Josh groaned. "That's *mental* enrichment, you idiot."

Andy grinned sheepishly. "Oops."

The red intercom button on the desk phone blinked. Blanco in our friend's body reached for it, but Josh in the principal's body slapped his hand away and answered it himself. "Yo, Mrs. Hub, wazup?"

"Oliver Hawkins is here to see you," she said.

"Send him in," said Josh in Blanco.

The door opened and Ollie came in with his petition.

"Hey, Ollie!" I gave him a high five.

"Hey, guys," he said. "What are you doing here?"

"Just hanging with good old Mr. Blanco," Andy said.

Ollie frowned.

"How can I help you, Hawkins?" Blanco in Josh asked.

"You can't help me, Josh," Ollie answered. "I'm here to see Principal Blanco."

On the other side of the desk, Josh in the principal's body grinned. "Yeah, Josh, you sniveling, lowly eighth grader, who do you think you are?"

Blanco in Josh pursed his lips angrily.

"Hey, Ollie," said Josh in Blanco's body. "What do you get when you cross a parrot with a centipede?"

"Gee, Principal Blanco, I don't know," Ollie replied.

"A walkie-talkie!" Josh in Blanco said.

Ollie smiled crookedly. "That's pretty funny, Principal Blanco."

"I used to take being principal very seriously, Ollie," Josh in Blanco said. "But I've turned over a new leaf. From now on, being principal is going to be one big joke. So what can I do for you?"

"Well, uh, me and my friends have been talking about this problem we have," Ollie began. "You see, my friends and I aren't the biggest kids around. In fact, we're kind of on the small side. I mean, I'm talking about kids like Howie Jamison and Joey Neves and Tyler Downs. And those are just my close friends. There are a lot of other small kids, too. Like Ricky Leeds and Dylan Fitzpatrick. And then there's — "

"Cut to the chase, Ollie," Josh in the principal's body interrupted. "I don't have time to listen to you name every shrimp in school."

"Oh, uh, okay, Principal Blanco," Ollie said. "You see, there are a lot of us smaller guys who really like to play sports. I like basketball, and so does Howie. And Tyler and Ricky are really into football, and Dylan — "

"You don't have to tell me what sport every kid likes to play," Josh in Blanco said irritably. "Get to the point, Ollie. Can't you see I'm a busy man?"

Ollie looked around the office. "Uh, no offense, Principal Blanco, but with your feet up on the desk and the music playing, you don't look very busy at all."

Josh in Blanco's body dropped his jaw. "Oh, yeah? Watch this." He pressed the red intercom button on the desk phone. "Mrs. Hub?"

"Yes, Principal Blanco," his secretary's voice crackled back.

"Put some calls through," Josh in the principal's body ordered.

"I would, sir, but no one's called," answered Mrs. Hub.

"Then *get* someone to call," Josh in Blanco's body ordered. He turned back to Ollie. "Where were we?"

"I was telling you who liked to play what sports," Ollie said. "And you told me to hurry because you were busy. And I said that you didn't really look very busy and you said — "

"Get to the point, Ollie!" Josh, Andy, and I all shouted at the same time.

Ollie looked surprised but then nodded. "Okay, well, basically me and my friends don't think it's fair that we're not big enough to get on the school teams."

Briiiiing! The desk phone rang.

"See," Josh in Blanco said to Ollie. "I *told* you I was busy." He pressed the red button. "Who's on the phone, Mrs. Hub?"

"Mr. Upchurch," Mrs. Hub reported.

"Who?" Josh in Blanco asked.

"The man who organizes the annual blood drive," Mrs. Hub said.

"Why is he on the phone?" asked Josh in the principal's body.

"Because you told me to have someone call you," Mrs. Hub answered.

"Try someone else," said Josh in Blanco. "Someone interesting."

Meanwhile, on our side of the desk, Blanco in Josh's body groaned wearily. "A twenty-year career, demolished in an instant!"

Josh in the principal's body turned back to Ollie. "Okay, so you don't think it's fair that you and your friends can't play on the school teams. What do you want me to do?"

"We want to start some new teams," Ollie said, holding up the pile of petitions. "I got all these kids and teachers to sign petitions for a basketball league for kids five foot six or shorter, and a new football league for kids who weigh a hundred and twenty pounds or less."

Ollie put the petitions on the desk. "I even

went around to some of the other middle schools and got the small guys there to sign up. So we know there's support for the idea at those schools, too."

"That's ridiculous," said Blanco in Josh's body. "You can't start new sports leagues with restrictions on weight and size. It's discriminatory."

"Says who, Josh?" Ollie argued. "They wrestle by weight class. Why can't we do the same thing in basketball and football?"

"Good point, Ollie!" Andy banged his fist against the desk.

"Forget it," said Blanco in Josh. "There's no money in the budget for new teams."

"How would you know, Josh?" Ollie asked.

"Yeah, *Josh*," agreed our friend in the principal's body. He turned to the computer. "I bet there's a lot of padding in the budget. Let's see what we can get rid of. The debating society. We don't need that." He started to type.

"What are you doing?" Blanco in Josh asked anxiously.

"Getting money for the shrimp league," answered Josh in Blanco.

"Oh, wow, Principal Blanco!" Ollie cried. "That's great! Thanks a bunch! Wait'll I tell my friends!"

"No sweat," replied Josh in the principal as he scrolled through the computer. "This is easy. It's like Simm School System. Do we really need the honor society? Forget it. The brainiacs already get more than they deserve. And home economics and woodworking. And the service club and the international club. And art. Who needs that?"

Blanco leaned Josh's body against the desk and shouted. *"You can't do this!"*

"Says who?" Josh in the principal's body shouted back.

Blanco in Josh leaned back in his chair and shook his head. "It's all ridiculous. All of that together isn't nearly enough to pay for sports teams."

"Hmmmm." Josh drummed the principal's fingers thoughtfully against the desk. "What else could we get rid of?"

With the radio turned low we could hear all kinds of screeches and annoying racket coming from the music room across the hall.

"Music!" Andy cried. "Let's get rid of that! And the band and orchestra. We could sell all the instruments. That would give the shrimp league plenty of money!"

"But you can't!" Blanco in Josh insisted.

Meanwhile, Josh in the principal's body typed on the computer. "Done."

The red intercom light on the phone blinked. Josh in Blanco pressed it. "Wazup, Mrs. Hub?"

"Ms. Rogers is here to see you," reported the secretary.

"Forget it," said Josh in Blanco. "I don't want

to see her." He turned to Ollie. "Okay, my friend. It's good-bye, music. Hello, shrimp sports league."

Suddenly the door swung open and Ms. Rogers stomped in. Her face was flushed and she looked really peeved.

15

"What is going on, Phil?" Ms. Rogers demanded. "I'd really like to know what this ridiculous nose and ear hair business is about."

Josh in the principal's body shot me a nervous look across the desk. No one knew what to say. We couldn't exactly tell her it was just an excuse to expel Barry Dunn.

"Hey, Ms. Rogers," Ollie suddenly piped up. "Want to hear something great?"

Ms. Rogers turned. "Oh, hello, Ollie. Sorry, I didn't see you."

"That's okay, Ms. Rogers," Ollie said. "People sometimes miss me in a crowd. But guess what Principal Blanco just did. He approved sports teams for small guys like me. He even got the money to pay for them."

Ms. Rogers turned back to Josh in the principal's body. Her expression changed. "Why, Phil, I'm delighted to hear that."

"Thank you," Josh in Blanco replied. "It simply wasn't fair the other way."

Ms. Rogers looked puzzled. "If you're trying to be fair, how can you justify expelling students because they have untrimmed nose hairs?"

"Guess you just have to take the bad with the good," Josh in Blanco replied with a shrug.

Ms. Rogers frowned as if she'd heard that before but couldn't remember where.

Briiing! The desk phone rang. Josh in Blanco reached forward and pressed the intercom button. "Wazup, Mrs. Hub?"

"I have a woman on the phone who says she can belly dance on a skateboard and juggle kittens at the same time."

"Why?" Josh in Blanco twisted his face into a scowl.

"You said you wanted to talk to someone interesting," Mrs. Hub said.

"Not *that* interesting." Josh in Blanco let go of the button and turned to our social studies teacher. "Is there anything else, Ms. Rogers?"

"Why are you calling me that?" Ms. Rogers asked. "You always call me Kim."

"Yes, of course, er, Kim," said Josh in the principal's body.

Ms. Rogers looked at her watch and started to get up. "I have to get to my next class. I just hope you'll reconsider this nose and ear hair business, Phil. It makes absolutely no sense."

Josh nodded Blanco's head, and Ms. Rogers left.

"Guess I better get going, too," said Ollie. "Thanks for the support, Principal Blanco. I can't wait to tell my friends."

"Piece of cake," replied Josh in Blanco.

As soon as Ollie left, Blanco crossed Josh's arms and glared across the desk. "Now what, *Mr. Principal?*"

Josh in the principal's body smiled and put his hands behind his head. "Now . . . we wait."

16

We spent the rest of the day in the principal's office listening to music and playing video games on his computer.

"Cool games, Principal Blanco," Andy said when it was his turn behind the computer.

"They came with the computer," Blanco in our friend's body grumbled. "I never play them."

"Then how come all these high score records have the initials PBB next to them?" Andy asked innocently.

"Isn't your name Philip Boynton Blanco?" I asked with a smile.

Blanco in Josh's body started to blush.

"Hey, come on, Mr. Blanco," I said. "Can't you loosen up a little and have some fun?"

"Running a school isn't *supposed* to be fun," Blanco in Josh snapped. "Dealing with characters like you and your friends isn't *fun*." He turned to Josh in the principal's body. "Excuse me for asking this, *Mr. Principal*, but shouldn't Andy and

Jake be in class instead of hanging around in here all day?"

"They can go to class tomorrow," Josh in the principal's body replied.

"Do we *have* to?" Andy and I asked in disappointment. "It's a lot more fun hanging around here and helping you run the school."

"True," Josh in Blanco agreed. "Maybe I will let you hang around again tomorrow."

"Yeah!" Andy and I cheered.

The bell rang. School was over.

"Okay, you three," said Josh in the principal's body. "Get out of here. I'll see you in the morning."

Andy frowned. "Aren't you going home, too?"

Josh shook Blanco's head. "I have to wait for the after-school programs to end and then lock up the school for the night."

That caught Andy and me by surprise. "Why?"

"I can't leave the school open all night," explained Josh in the principal's body. "It would be irresponsible."

We were shocked. "*You* don't have to be responsible for that," I said, then pointed at Blanco in Josh's body. "Let *him* do it."

"Did it ever occur to you that people might get a little suspicious if they saw Josh Hopka locking up the school tonight?" Josh in the principal's body replied.

"Why not?" Blanco in Josh asked with a rueful

laugh. "If the principal can wear tattoos and order nostril hair inspections, why *shouldn't* he also let an eighth grader lock up?"

"I'm locking up tonight," Josh in the principal's body insisted. "End of discussion!"

"Uh, okay," Andy allowed uncomfortably. "Come on, guys, I guess we can go."

"I suppose I should be thankful for small favors," muttered Blanco in Josh's body as he got up. "Just promise me that you won't get any more tattoos."

"I promise," replied Josh in the principal's body. "Tonight I'm going to get some earrings. And maybe get my belly button pierced."

Blanco in Josh bit his lip. "You're joking, right?"

Josh took out the principal's gold Visa card again and smiled. Blanco in our friend's body turned to Andy and me with a pale, desperate look. "Andy, Jake, tell me he's joking."

"I think he's serious," I said.

"I bet he wants to do it to your body because his parents won't let him do it to *his*," added Andy.

A look of terror came over our friend's face as Blanco realized Josh was serious. "You can't have my body pierced!"

"Promise you'll expel Barry Dunn," said Andy.

"I . . . I can't!" Blanco in our friend's body answered woefully. "Try to understand. It's not that

I don't *want* to expel him. But there are rules and procedures that must be followed."

Josh in Blanco's body turned to Andy and me. "How about a gold hoop right through the eyebrow? Or one of those tongue studs?"

We looked at Principal Blanco in Josh's body, wondering if that would get him to change his mind.

Blanco shook Josh's head wearily. "I can't break the rules. It's not fair. Go ahead, Josh. Do whatever you want to my body."

Head hanging, he trudged out of the office.

"Talk about a principal with principles," Andy said. "I don't think we'll ever get him to change his mind and expel Barry."

"Doesn't matter," said Josh in the principal's body. "Now that I'm the principal, I'll get rid of Barry."

Josh in the principal's body followed Andy and me out of his office. Out in the main office, Mrs. Hub was on the phone. She put her hand over the receiver. "Mr. Blanco?"

"Yes, Mrs. Hub?" replied Josh in Blanco's body.

"I have the Vice President of the United States on the phone," Mrs. Hub said.

Josh in Blanco's body frowned. "Why?"

"Well, you said you wanted someone interesting but not too interesting," Mrs. Hub explained.

"Oh, all right," answered Josh in Blanco's body. "Tell him to hold."

Josh in Blanco's body came out into the hall with Andy and me. "Okay, boys, see you tomorrow."

"Sure." As Andy and I turned to go, a couple of sixth graders ran past us.

"No running in the halls!" Josh in the principal's body barked.

Both kids instantly slowed down.

"That's better," said Josh in Blanco's body and went back into the office.

Andy and I shared an uncomfortable look.

"You get the feeling something weird is going on?" Andy asked as we left school. "Like the way he insisted on locking up tonight and told those kids to stop running?"

"It's like sometimes he forgets he's Josh and starts to think he really *is* the principal," I said.

"Exactly," said Andy. We got off school property and started down the street.

"Well, well," a voice suddenly said. "Look who's here."

Andy and I spun around. Coming out from behind a tree was Barry Dunn.

17

A ndy and I froze.

Barry gave Andy a nasty grin. "If it ain't Mr. My-girlfriend's-best-friend's-boyfriend-is-Snakebite-McGuinn."

"It's *Sharkbait McGuire*," I corrected him. "And he's the best friend of the boyfriend of my sister's best friend."

"Who cares?" Barry scoffed.

"I bet Sharkbait McGuire does," Andy said nervously. "I mean, would you want to be called Snakebite if your nickname was really Sharkbait?"

"They're both better than Dead Meat, which is what you'll be calling that twirp Josh when I get finished with him," Barry growled. He looked around. "So where is he, anyway?"

Andy and I shared a nervous glance. We knew that Blanco in Josh's body had already left school. He must have taken the school bus home.

"Uh, I think he's still at school," I answered, winking at Andy.

"Yeah." Andy quickly caught on. "In fact, he'll probably come right down this street pretty soon."

Barry grinned. "Good. Don't tell him I'm here." He went back and hid behind the tree.

Andy and I continued down the road from school. As soon as we were out of earshot, Andy turned to me.

"I just had a scary thought," he said. "I imagined Barry Dunn *with brains*."

I felt a chill run through me. "You're right, Andy. That *is* scary."

18

The next morning Josh in Blanco's body was standing outside of the front doors before school began. Unlike the cool clothes he'd worn the day before, today he was wearing a dark suit just like the real Principal Blanco might have worn. A bunch of small, round, pink Band-Aids dotted his jaw and neck.

"What's with the suit?" Andy asked as we walked toward him.

"It projects the right image of authority," Josh in Blanco replied.

" 'Image of authority'?" I repeated. "What do you need *that* for?"

"Someone has to run the school while we try to get rid of Barry," Josh in the principal replied.

Andy and I shared a wary look. Josh in Principal Blanco was starting to sound more and more like a principal and less and less like our friend.

"What's with the Band-Aids?" Andy asked.

"I, uh, cut myself shaving," answered Josh in Blanco.

"Why'd you want to shave?" I asked.

"You didn't expect me to come to school unshaven, did you?" Josh in Blanco asked.

The bell rang.

"Okay, everyone," Josh in Blanco shouted to a bunch of kids loitering outside the building. "It's time to go inside!"

The kids obeyed as if they believed it really was Principal Blanco speaking to them. Andy and I walked with Josh in the principal's body into the building.

"So this is it," Andy said eagerly. "The day we get rid of Barry Dunn for good! Listen, Josh, as soon as we get to the office, you can call him down, check his nostril hairs, and expel him forever."

Our friend in Blanco's body hesitated. "I don't know about that, Andy."

"What are you talking about?" Andy asked. "That's the whole idea. That's why you switched with Principal Blanco in the first place. That's why I got all those kids to cut your lawn for the next two years."

Josh in Blanco straightened the sleeves of his suit. "I know that, Andy. But if I just call Barry down and expel him, it's going to look too obvious. I think I should call someone else down and expel that kid first. Then it won't look like I was just doing this to get Barry."

"Who do you want to expel?" I asked.

"Someone you wouldn't expect," Josh in Blanco said. "A real obnoxious goody-two-shoes teacher's pet."

At the same time, Andy and I said, "Amanda Gluck!"

Even Josh in Blanco's body smiled. "Perfect!"

We went into the main office. Blanco in Josh was waiting there for us. Once again, he was wearing the nerdiest clothes he could find in Josh's closet — a long-sleeved yellow button-down shirt and brown slacks with cuffs. This time, however, Josh didn't seem to notice.

Mrs. Hub looked up from her desk.

"Good morning, Mr. Blanco, a Mr. Petersen from the state education department just called," she said, handing Josh in the principal's body some pink phone memos. "He wants you to call him right away. And here's a message from the blood drive people."

"Right." Josh in Blanco took the pink slips.

Meanwhile, Mrs. Hub gave him a concerned look. "Excuse me for asking this, sir, but what happened to your face?"

"I cut myself shaving," Josh in Blanco replied.

"But you shave every morning," Mrs. Hub pointed out, "and you've never cut yourself before."

"Well, uh, this morning the razor was really sharp," Josh in Blanco tried to explain. "Anyway, have Amanda Gluck come to my office immediately."

Josh in the principal's body turned to Blanco in Josh. "Why aren't you in class, son?"

Blanco in Josh darted his eyes toward Mrs. Hub. "Oh, uh, I have to talk to you about something *in private*."

"Yeah, right," Josh in Blanco smirked and went into his office. Andy, Blanco in Josh, and I followed. As soon as Josh in Blanco's body closed the office door, he crumpled up the pink phone memos and shot them into the wastepaper can.

"You can't do that!" protested Blanco in our friend's body.

"Why not?" said Josh in the principal's body.

"One of those messages was someone from the state education department," said Josh in Blanco. "It could be important."

"To *you* maybe," Josh in Blanco replied. "Not to me."

"I'm sure it's about the tests you took," said Blanco in Josh. "The grading is all computerized now. They get the results back very quickly."

"Hey, I want to know how I did," I said. "Call him back, Josh."

Josh in the principal's body reached into the wastepaper basket and uncrumpled one of the pink memos. Then he dialed the phone number.

"Mr. Petersen?" he said. "This is Principal Blanco from the Burp It Up, er, I mean, Burt

Itchupt Middle School. I'm returning your phone call."

We watched as Josh in Blanco listened. His eyes widened, and he grabbed a pen and started taking notes. "You don't say? Yes, it's very interesting. Yes, I see your point. I'll get on it right away. Of course. And good day to you, too, Mr. Petersen."

Josh in Blanco hung up.

"What did he say?" asked Blanco in our friend's body.

"We did better than the state average," Josh in the principal's body answered. "And Amber Sweeny and Howie Jamison got two of the highest scores ever recorded. Mr. Petersen suggested that they both be skipped immediately to ninth grade."

"You'd better call their parents and have them come in right away," advised Blanco in Josh. "If they're going to move up to the high school it has to be done fast. You don't want them to skip a grade and then find that they're behind the other students."

"Right." Josh in Blanco pressed the intercom button on the phone. "Mrs. Hub, please call Amber Sweeny's and Howie Jamison's parents and have them come to school for a meeting as soon as possible."

"I will, sir," Mrs. Hub replied. "And Amanda Gluck is here to see you."

"Very good," Josh in Blanco replied. "Send her in and call Barry Dunn down to the office."

Josh in Blanco took his finger off the intercom button. The door opened and Amanda Gluck came in, looking very nervous. She scowled when she saw all the Band-Aids on the principal's face.

Josh in the principal's body gestured to the empty chair on the other side of his desk. "Have a seat, Amanda."

Amanda sat down. Josh in Blanco cupped his hands pensively and leaned his elbows on the desk. "Amanda, I'm afraid I have some bad news. I'm going to have to expel you."

Amanda's mouth fell open in shock. "Why?"

"Untrimmed nostril hairs," Josh in the principal's body said solemnly.

"But . . . you didn't even look!" Amanda argued.

"I don't have to look," Josh in Blanco replied.

"What am I going to tell my parents?" Amanda asked.

"Tell them there are places for people like you, Amanda," Josh in Blanco said. "Places where kids have dress codes and take time to brush their teeth after every meal. I suggest you and your parents seek them out. You may go."

In a daze, Amanda got up and left the office.

"You're going to pay for that," Blanco in Josh growled.

"No, *you* are," replied Josh in Blanco with a grin.

The red intercom button on the desk phone flashed. "Barry Dunn is here to see you, sir."

Josh in Blanco smiled. "Send him right in."

The door opened, and Barry stepped into the office, looking surly. He narrowed his eyes menacingly at Blanco in Josh.

"Have a seat, Dunn," ordered Josh in the principal's body.

Barry frowned and slouched down in a chair. "What's with your face?"

"Bullet wounds," Josh in the principal's body snapped irritably.

Barry smirked and looked at Andy, Blanco in Josh, and me. "What're all these guys doing here?" he asked.

"We're the principal's posse," Andy announced brightly.

Barry rolled his eyes in disbelief and turned to Josh in Blanco. "I saw your tattoos yesterday, Mr. Blanco. You get them at the Body Art Bodega or Piercings Plus?"

"Actually, I got them at the Tattoo Trattoria," Josh in Blanco's body replied. "But we're not here to talk about tattoos, Dunn. We're here to talk about nostril hairs."

To our surprise, Barry reached into his pocket, took out a small magnifying glass, and handed it across the desk to Josh in the principal's body. Then he tilted back his head. "Go ahead, Mr. Blanco, have a look."

19

Josh furrowed Principal Blanco's forehead deeply. I could see that inside the principal's body, my friend was sharing the same confusion I felt. Why was Barry inviting him to look up his nose?

Josh in Blanco picked up the magnifying glass, leaned across the desk, and carefully inspected Barry's nostrils.

A moment later he slumped back into the principal's chair.

"So?" Andy asked eagerly.

"Clean as a whistle," Josh in Blanco's body admitted with a sigh.

"Not a *single* unruly nostril hair?" Andy asked in amazement.

Josh shook Blanco's head. "They're perfectly trimmed."

"How about boogers?" Andy asked desperately.

"Excuse me," Blanco in Josh interrupted, "but

if you could get expelled for boogers, this school would be empty."

Barry grinned triumphantly. "I knew what you were trying to do when you made that dumb nostril hair rule, Principal Blanco. You were just looking for a way to kick me out of school. But I was too smart for you. You're gonna have to think up something a lot smarter than that if you want to catch me. I mean, I know I used to do dumb stuff, but now I — "

"Are you done?" Josh in Blanco's body asked impatiently.

"You know I'm Dunn," Barry replied. "But I was just saying that maybe I used to do dumb stuff, but I really wised up. I'm a lot smarter than I — "

"I said, are you done?" Josh in Blanco repeated.

Barry frowned. "Of course I'm Dunn. You just can't believe it because I outsmarted you. You're just like these guys." Barry pointed at Andy, Blanco in Josh, and me. "You think I'm just an overgrown troll with the mental capacity of a pothole."

"Speed bump," Andy corrected him.

"Uh, right." Barry nodded. "That's what I meant. Well, maybe I *used* to be that dumb, but now I'm smart. I know which end is up and what putrification means. I know — "

"Are you done?" Josh in Blanco interrupted for a third time.

Barry frowned. "You *know* that's my name.

What's wrong with you? Did you take a stupid pill this morning or something?"

"That's it!" Josh banged Blanco's hand against the desktop. "I've had about all the insubordination I can stand from you, Dunn. You're expelled!"

"All right!" Andy raised his fist in triumph.

Barry's jaw dropped. "You can't!"

"Oh, yes, I can, Dunn!" Josh in Blanco's body yelled. "Now get out of here!"

Barry got up and retreated to the door. "You tricked me! You can't get away with this, Mr. Blanco. I'm gonna tell my parents."

"Go ahead." Josh in Blanco's body waved him away. "Tell the world."

Bang! Barry slammed the door closed behind him.

Andy jumped out of his seat and did a dance around the principal's office. "We did it! Oh, yeah! We're cool! We got rid of Big Bad Dunn! Ya-hoo! Stick a fork in him, *he's Dunn!*"

Josh in Blanco's body smiled and leaned back in his chair. "Now I don't have to cut my lawn for two years!"

I turned to look at Blanco in Josh's body. His face was red and his fists were clenched. In fact, he looked like he was ready to explode.

"Ahem!" I cleared my throat. "Guys?"

Andy stopped dancing. Josh in Blanco stopped grinning.

Blanco in our friend's body jumped to his feet. "You've undermined my authority!" He screamed across the desk. "You've broken my word. You've ruined my reputation. You've . . . given me ugly tattoos and made me eat warm, mushy, peanut-butter-and-jelly sandwiches! *I'll kill you!*"

With a mad glint in his eye, Blanco in Josh lunged across the desk!

"Get him away from me!" Josh in Blanco screamed.

Andy and I grabbed Blanco in Josh and started to wrestle him to the floor.

"I'll get you!" Blanco in Josh screamed and struggled. "I swear! If it's the last thing I do!"

Andy and I forced Blanco in Josh down to the floor and sat on him. Just then the office door swung open and Mrs. Hub came in. "What in the world is going on?"

20

Still sitting on Blanco in our friend's body, Andy and I looked quickly to Josh in the principal's body.

"Oh, uh, it's nothing, Mrs. Hub," Josh in Blanco said. "The boys were just demonstrating a new form of yoga."

"Sitting on each other?" Mrs. Hub asked, puzzled.

"He's not me!" Blanco in Josh suddenly screamed from under Andy and me. "He's — *mmmph!*"

He couldn't finish talking because I quickly covered his mouth with my hand.

"What was that?" Mrs. Hub asked. "It sounded like he said you weren't him."

Blanco in Josh twisted and squirmed under Andy and me, but we held him down and I kept my hand over his mouth.

"Sometimes they shout strange things while

they're trying to relax," Josh in the principal's body explained.

"He doesn't look very relaxed," Mrs. Hub observed.

"Hopka's a tough nut to crack," Josh in Blanco agreed. "But I'm confident we'll succeed. By the way, Mrs. Hub, what brings you in here?"

Mrs. Hub pointed at the desk phone. The red intercom light was blinking. "You weren't answering your intercom."

"Ah, I see," said Josh in Blanco. "I guess we were all too busy with the yoga. What were you buzzing me about, Mrs. Hub?"

"The main office is filling with parents who want to see you," Mrs. Hub explained. "And the man from McDonald's is here about the new school lunch program. There's no place left for them to sit. I suggest you start seeing them."

"*MMMMMMmmmmmmmm! MMmmmmmmm!*" Blanco in Josh started to squirm and shake his head. Andy and I had to press down harder to keep him from escaping.

"Uh, yes, of course," Josh in the principal replied. "I'll get to them in a moment. Thank you, Mrs. Hub."

The white-haired secretary left the office.

"*MMMMMMmmmmmmmm! MMmmmmmmm!*" Blanco in Josh kept struggling. I kept my hand over his mouth.

"Let's hear what he has to say," said Josh in Blanco.

I took my hand off Josh's mouth.

"You can't meet with those parents!" Blanco in Josh cried. "You don't know what to say. You don't know how to handle them. You'll only make a mess of things and do even more damage to my reputation."

Josh in Blanco's body pressed a finger thoughtfully against his lips. "You're probably right. I probably *will* destroy your reputation. . . . But I think I'll meet with them anyway."

"No!" Blanco in our friend's body started to squirm and twist even harder. Andy and I were having a hard time holding him down.

"You have to do something," I told Josh in Blanco. "You can't meet with the parents while he's thrashing around like this."

Josh pointed Blanco's finger at the principal in our friend's body. "Listen up, Mr. Blanco. You better not make any trouble for us. You may think your reputation's in bad shape now, but believe me, you haven't seen anything."

Blanco in Josh's body stopped struggling. "What more could you do?"

"I could call the whole school into another assembly and then demonstrate my unique ability to juggle overripe tomatoes and blow spit bubbles at the same time," answered Josh in the principal's body.

Our friend's face went pale as Blanco realized Josh wasn't kidding.

"What should we do with him?" Andy asked Josh in the principal's body.

"Get him out of here," replied Josh in Blanco. "I've got important meetings."

21

Andy and I hustled Blanco in Josh out of the principal's office. Mrs. Hub wasn't kidding when she said the main office was filled with parents waiting to see Blanco. On the way out I recognized Amber Sweeny's parents and Howie Jamison's. I'd never seen Amanda Gluck's parents before, but I figured they were the neatly dressed ones with the thick eyeglasses who were sitting with Amanda. I'd never seen Barry Dunn's parents either, but there was no mistaking the man with the greasy T-shirt and blond ponytail or the bored-looking woman with bright red hair who was chewing gum and filing her nails. They were sitting with Barry, who sneered at us as we passed.

We left the main office.

"What were Amanda's and Barry's parents doing in there?" Andy asked.

"They're there because their kids have been expelled from school for the most illogical reasons in the world," Blanco in Josh answered bitterly. "They won't stand for it. I told you this inane plan of yours would never work."

Andy and I shared a nervous glance.

"I think we better go to class," I said.

We started down the hall. Classes had just changed, and social studies was about to begin, so we headed for Ms. Rogers's room. Just before we got there Blanco in our friend's body suddenly stopped.

"Hear that?" he asked.

"What?" Andy said.

"Listen," said Blanco in Josh.

Andy and I stopped and listened. We could hear the faint sound of water splashing. Blanco in Josh looked around, then pointed at the boys' room. Water was seeping out from under the door and into the hallway.

The next thing we knew, Blanco in our friend's body pushed open the boys' room door and splashed through the water on the floor inside. A moment later he came out. His shoes and the bottoms of his pants were soaked.

"Darn it!" he grumbled. "They did it again!"

He hurried across the hall and pushed open the door to Ms. Rogers's room. Inside, Ms. Rogers looked shocked as Blanco in Josh's body grabbed the wall phone.

"What do you think you're doing?" Ms. Rogers demanded.

"Just a second, Kim," Blanco in Josh replied. Then he spoke into the phone. "Mrs. Hub, this is Phil. Find Dave Phelps and get him over to the eighth-grade wing fast. They've flooded the boys' room again. . . . What? Yes, I know Principal Blanco is in his office. But he's not the principal. I am!"

"Get off the phone, Josh," Ms. Rogers ordered.

But Blanco in Josh was still arguing with Mrs. Hub.

"You don't believe I'm the principal?" Blanco in Josh growled into the phone. "Then go in Blanco's office and tell *him* to get Dave Phelps!"

Meanwhile, Ms. Rogers crossed her arms. "This is the last time I'm going to tell you to get off that phone, Josh."

Blanco in our friend's body hung up the phone and shook his head. "I can't believe this is happening," he muttered. "It's like a nightmare."

"I can't understand what's gotten into you, Josh," Ms. Rogers said.

"What's gotten into me?" Josh repeated with a bitter laugh in front of the whole class. "I'll tell you what's gotten into me. An eighth-grade *maniac* has gotten into me. And what's worse is that I'm stuck in him!"

"What?" Ms. Rogers frowned.

"Don't forget spit bubbles and overripe tomato juggling," Andy reminded Blanco in our friend's body.

"Spit bubbles and overripe tomato juggling?" Ms. Rogers repeated. "What is going on?"

Before we could make up an excuse, the wall phone rang. Blanco in Josh's body started to reach for it.

"It's not for you," Ms. Rogers said in a scolding tone and reached for the phone. "Hello? Yes, Mrs. Hub. Uh-huh. Yes, I see. All right, I'll send them right down."

Our social studies teacher hung up the phone and turned to the class. "Amber and Howie, Principal Blanco wants you to come down to his office immediately."

With puzzled expressions on their faces, Amber Sweeny and Howie Jamison got up and left the classroom. Andy, Blanco in Josh, and I sat down. Our seats were near the windows.

"All right, class," Ms. Rogers said. "Let's get back to the Bill of Rights. Who knows what the Eighth Amendment says?"

The first hand to go up belonged to Julia Sax. "The Eighth Amendment states that excessive bail shall not be required, nor excessive fines imposed, nor cruel and unusual punishments inflicted."

"Who can give me an example?" Ms. Rogers asked.

Blanco in Josh's body immediately raised his hand.

"Yes, Josh?" Ms. Rogers said.

"Being expelled from school for having untrimmed nostril hairs," Blanco in our friend's body said.

"Amen," Ms. Rogers said with a smile.

I felt someone poke me in the back. It was Andy, who sat behind me. "Jake," he hissed. "Look outside."

I looked out. Going down the walk away from school were Howie Jamison, Barry Dunn, Amanda Gluck, and their parents. As you might expect, Howie's parents were smiling at the news that he'd just been skipped ahead to ninth grade. And Amanda's parents were upset that Amanda had been expelled for untrimmed nostril hairs.

The weird thing was that Barry and his parents were all smiling. Barry's father was even patting him on the back.

"How can they be happy about Barry being expelled?" Andy whispered.

I couldn't answer that. Nor could I explain what we saw next: Amber Sweeny and her parents came out of school. Mrs. Sweeny was dabbing her eyes with a tissue. Mr. Sweeny looked grim. Amber trudged behind them with her shoulders stooped and her eyes to the ground.

Back in the classroom, Blanco in Josh glanced outside and saw Amber and her parents. "Oh, no!" he cried and jumped up from his seat.

"What are you doing, Josh?" Ms. Rogers asked.

Blanco in our friend's body didn't answer. Instead he dashed toward the door.

"Josh, you do not have permission to leave this room!" Ms. Rogers said sternly.

But Blanco in Josh pulled open the door and ran out.

Ms. Rogers sighed wearily. "I wish someone would tell me what's going on." She turned her gaze to Andy and me. "I've interrupted this class enough today. I'm not going to do it again. Jake and Andy, go out in the hall and bring your friend Josh back here immediately."

"Yes, ma'am." Andy and I jumped up and left.

By the time we got out to the hall, Blanco in our friend's body had almost reached the main office. We raced to catch up to him and all entered the office at the same time.

Mrs. Hub looked up at us and frowned. "What are you doing here?"

"I'll bet that idiot doesn't even know what he did," Blanco in Josh's body grumbled as he headed for the principal's office.

"You can't just barge in there!" Mrs. Hub said.

"Try and stop me." Blanco in Josh yanked open the principal's door and stormed in.

Mrs. Hub turned to Andy and me. "And where do you two think you're going?"

"We want to see if the idiot knows what he did," Andy answered as we followed Blanco in

Josh's body into the principal's office. Josh in the principal's body was sitting behind the desk, trying to fix one of his cuff links.

"Do you have any idea what you just did?" Blanco in our friend's body asked.

"Sure, I just messed up this cuff link," replied Josh in the principal's body.

"No! I mean *before* that."

Josh in the principal's body frowned. "Before that I went to the bathroom."

"No! *Before* that!"

"Before that?" Josh scratched Blanco's head. "I guess I was thinking about going to the bathroom."

"No! I mean, when you talked to the parents!" yelled Blanco in our friend's body. "Did you have the parents come in here with their kids?"

"No," answered Josh in the principal's body. "The kids stayed outside. I wanted to talk to the parents in private."

"I knew it!" Blanco in our friend's body cried.

"How?" asked Josh in the principal's body.

"Because you got the parents mixed up, you idiot! You *expelled* Amber Sweeny, and you moved Barry Dunn up to ninth grade!"

On the other side of the desk, Josh widened Blanco's eyes. "Ooops!"

"I'll say oops!" Blanco in Josh snarled. "Not only have you royally messed up *their* lives, but you've made me look like an even bigger idiot!"

"Hey! It's not easy to have all these meetings," Josh in the principal's body shot back. "I don't know who all these parents are. So *excuuuuuse* me if I mixed a few of them up."

"No, you're not excused," Blanco in our friend's body snapped. "You'd better get on the phone right now and fix it."

"Okay, okay, you don't have to be so pushy." Josh in the principal's body shrank back and reached for the phone. "It was just a *little* mix-up."

"Oh, sure," Blanco in Josh's body said angrily. "Expelling the best student in the eighth grade for no reason. That's not what I call a *little* mix-up."

"Just chill, I'm calling Amber's house right now," Josh in Blanco said, then spoke into the phone. "Hello? Is anyone there? This is Principal Blanco from the middle school. I'm calling because the computer made a terrible error. The RAM in the windows gigged when it should have megged, and the motherboard deleted the baby on board. But it's all been fixed and I have good news. Amber wasn't supposed to be expelled. She was supposed to be skipped into ninth grade. So, uh, when you get this message, please give me a call, okay? Thanks, bye."

Josh in the principal's body hung up the phone. "I left a message. See how easy it was to fix? What's the big deal?"

"That may have been easy," replied Blanco in Josh's body. "But now you have to tell the Dunns that instead of being skipped ahead a grade, their son has been expelled."

Josh in Blanco frowned and stared down at the phone. He took a deep breath and reached for the receiver.

That's when Andy suddenly shouted, "Wait!"

22

"Why wait?" asked Blanco in Josh's body.

"Don't call the Dunns," Andy said.

"But I have to," said Josh in the principal's body. "He's not supposed to go to ninth grade. He's supposed to be expelled."

"This is better!" Andy argued. "Let Barry go into ninth grade. That way we get rid of him and Josh doesn't have the hassle of having to prove why he should be expelled."

"He's right!" I realized. "This is *way* better."

"Way to go, Andy!" Josh held up Blanco's hand for a high five and Andy slapped it.

"But that's absurd!" Blanco in Josh's body sputtered. "Barry Dunn doesn't belong in ninth grade. He's barely capable of doing work on an eighth-grade level."

"Let the high school principal deal with it," shrugged Josh in the principal's body. He held out his arm. "Who can help me with this cuff link?"

"This is ridiculous!" Blanco in our friend's body jumped up. *Bang!* He left the office and slammed the door behind him.

The red intercom light on the phone flashed. Josh in the principal's body answered it. "Yes, Mrs. Hub?"

"Ms. Rogers is here," reported the secretary.

"Uh, tell her I'm busy," Josh in Blanco replied.

"She's saying something about your open-door policy," Mrs. Hub replied.

"Tell her I'm citing the Fourth Amendment," Josh in the principal's body replied. "The right of people to be secure in their offices against unreasonable searches."

"She says she's citing the Sixth Amendment," Mrs. Hub answered over the intercom. "The guarantee of basic procedural rights."

Josh in Blanco looked across the desk at Andy and I. "Got any ideas, guys?"

We shook our heads.

Our friend in the principal's body sighed and turned to the intercom. "All right, Mrs. Hub, send her in."

The door opened and Ms. Rogers came in. "What happened to your face?"

"Big zits," replied Josh in the principal's body.

Ms. Rogers gave Andy and me a puzzled look and turned to Josh in Blanco. "Phil, I sent Andy and Jake to get Josh. But I just saw Josh in the hall. Why are Andy and Jake still in your office?"

"I'm discussing important school policy," Josh in Blanco replied.

"With eighth graders?" Ms. Rogers asked.

"I need their input," explained Josh in Blanco.

"It seems like they're both spending an awful lot of time in this office lately," our teacher pointed out. "Aren't you concerned about all the class time they're missing?"

Before Josh in the principal's body could answer, the intercom light flashed again. Josh in Blanco's body pushed the button. "What now, Mrs. Hub?"

"I'm sorry to bother you, sir, but I just got a call from the cafetorium," Mrs. Hub reported. "It appears that Josh Hopka is creating some kind of commotion. They want you down there right away."

23

Ms. Rogers, Josh in the principal's body, Andy, and I hurried down to the cafetorium. In the middle of the room, Blanco in Josh's body was standing on a lunch table. Everyone around him was hiding under tables or crouching behind chairs. Not far from us, Ollie Hawkins cowered behind a garbage can.

"What's going on?" Josh in the principal's body asked him.

"Josh has gone wacko, Mr. Blanco," Ollie answered. "He's hitting everyone with peanut-butter-and-jelly bombs and he keeps yelling that he wants to be expelled."

"You'd better take care of this," Ms. Rogers told Josh in Blanco's body.

"Yes, er, absolutely," Josh in Blanco replied in a very uncertain tone.

Splat! A gooey wad of peanut-butter-and-jelly sandwich smacked the wall near us.

"Hey, Principal Blanco, you big jerk!" Blanco in

our friend's body shouted. "Come and get me! Expel me! I'm standing on a lunch table! I'm throwing food! I'm calling you names! And look!" Blanco pulled Josh's nostrils wide. "I've got untrimmed nostril hairs! I'm a walking, talking violation of school rules! You have to get rid of me!"

Josh in Blanco's body didn't budge.

"Why aren't you doing anything?" Ms. Rogers asked him.

Josh made Blanco's eyes dart back and forth. He was in a tough spot. How could he expel himself?

Meanwhile, Blanco in Josh tore off another glob of peanut-butter-and-jelly sandwich and threw it.

Splat! It hit Josh in Blanco right in the forehead.

"Hey, check it out!" Blanco in our friend's body shouted gleefully. "Now the outside of Principal Blanco's head looks exactly like what's inside! Come on, peanut-butter-and-jelly brains, aren't you going to expel me?"

"What are you waiting for?" Ms. Rogers asked Josh in the principal's body while he wiped peanut butter and jelly off his forehead with a handkerchief.

By now the rest of the cafetorium was also staring at Josh in Blanco, waiting to see what he'd do.

"I don't know why you're not doing anything,

Phil," Ms. Rogers said. "You can't let Josh do this to you. He's undermining your authority."

"Hey, everyone!" Blanco in Josh's body yelled from on top of the lunch table. "Listen to this! Principal Blanco was really cranko. He went to the banko in a tanko. He ate a ginkgo on toasted pinkgo, then burped a stinko and said 'I blinko.' "

Blanco in Josh's body tore off another hunk of peanut-butter-and-jelly sandwich and threw it.

Plop! It landed on Josh in Blanco's shoe, but he still didn't budge.

"This is ridiculous!" Ms. Rogers grumbled at Josh in the principal's body. "If you won't do anything, then I will!"

Ms. Rogers started toward the lunch table where Blanco in Josh was standing.

"Uh-oh! Look!" Blanco in our friend's body cried gleefully. "It's Ms. Rogers! Champion of small athletes! Defender of the shrimp league!" He tore off another piece of soggy peanut-butter-and-jelly sandwich and wound up to throw it at her.

"Stop!" Josh in Blanco suddenly bellowed.

The cafetorium went silent. Even Blanco in Josh's body looked surprised.

Josh in the principal's body pointed an angry finger. "If you throw that peanut butter and jelly at Ms. Rogers I'll make you go to class! I'll make you eat in the cafetoruim! I'll . . . I'll make you use *the boys' bathroom!*"

Blanco lowered Josh's arm. "You wouldn't dare!"

"I swear I will!" Josh in the principal's body promised.

"What are you both talking about?" Ms. Rogers asked. "Josh is *supposed* to go to class and eat in the cafetorium and use the boys' room. What kind of punishment is that?"

"The worst I can think of," Josh in Blanco's body answered.

Ms. Rogers looked completely bewildered. "Will someone *please* tell me what's going on?" she wailed.

My friends and I shared a look with Blanco in Josh's body.

"I have a feeling," I said, "that it's time to have a meeting."

24

Blanco in Josh's body climbed down and sat with us at the lunch table. All around the cafetorium kids began to crawl out from under tables and behind chairs as lunch returned to normal.

Meanwhile, Ms. Rogers still looked totally bewildered. "I don't understand."

"Don't worry, Kim," Josh in Blanco's body reassured her. "Everything's under control."

"If you say so, Phil." Still scowling, Ms. Rogers left the cafetorium.

Soon it was lunch as usual in the cafetorium. Kids were back in their seats eating and talking loudly. Hardly anyone paid attention to Blanco in Josh, Josh in Blanco, Andy, or me.

"Look, guys," I said. "I think we've lost sight of what our original goal was. The whole idea was to get rid of Barry Dunn, and we did that. I don't see why Principal Blanco can't have his body back."

"Maybe I don't want to give it back," said Josh in Blanco. "Maybe I *like* being principal."

"That's the sickest thing I ever heard," Andy muttered. "How could anyone like being a principal?"

"Hey, watch it!" warned Blanco in Josh's body. "Some people are proud to be principals. They work their whole careers to become one."

"Besides," added Josh in the principal's body, "did either of you boneheads ever stop to think about what's going to happen when Principal Blanco gets his body back? He's gonna expel us forever."

Andy and I gave Blanco in our friend's body a wary look.

"Swear we'll get amnesty," I said.

"I'll swear no such thing," huffed Blanco in Josh's body. "Thanks to you boys my reputation has been severely damaged. You've made me look like a fool and an idiot. As soon as I become principal again I intend to make sure each of you is severely punished."

I turned to Andy. "What are we going to do?"

"I know!" Andy jumped up. "Be right back."

He raced out of the cafetorium. A few moments later he was back with a computer disk. He held it up in front of the principal in Josh's body. "This is a copy of all the games you've got on your computer and what your scores were. If you do anything to us I'll send this disk to that guy in the state education department and tell him this is how you spend your time."

Blanco in Josh's body turned pale. "You wouldn't!"

"Try me." Andy dared him.

"Oh, no." Blanco in our friend's body groaned. "That would *really* be the end of my career."

"Then promise you won't do anything to us when we switch you back," I said.

Blanco nodded Josh's head reluctantly. "Okay. I promise. You have my word."

Andy and I turned to Josh in the principal's body. "It's settled. We're switching you back."

Josh jutted Blanco's chin out defiantly. "Make me."

I turned to Principal Blanco in our friend's body. "Excuse me, Mr. Blanco, but aren't you always the first to give blood in the annual blood drive each year?"

"Absolutely," answered Blanco in Josh. "As the head of this school, it is my job to set an example for the staff and faculty. I always go first."

"And when does the annual blood drive begin?" I asked.

Blanco checked the date on Josh's watch. "First thing tomorrow morning."

Andy and I turned to Josh in the principal's

body. "First thing tomorrow morning you're giving blood."

Now it was time for Josh in Blanco to turn pale. "With a needle?"

Andy nodded. "A long, *sharp* needle."

25

We agreed to meet after school in Mr. Dirksen's lab. When the final bell rang, Andy, Blanco in our friend's body, and I started toward the science wing.

"I can't wait to get out of this body," Blanco in Josh muttered in a low voice. "This has been the worst forty-eight hours of my life."

"Wasn't there anything good about it?" Andy asked.

"Let's see," Blanco in Josh mused. "I watched my career and reputation nearly get destroyed. I had to endure almost nonstop abuse from you two. And I had to consume soggy peanut-butter-and-jelly sandwiches at every meal. Nope, to tell you the truth, Andy, I can't think of one good thing about it."

In the hall ahead of us, Amber Sweeny was taking some books out of her locker.

"Hey, Amber," I said. "I thought you moved up to the ninth grade."

Amber swept back her long brown hair and shook her head. "Principal Blanco said I had a choice. I decided not to do it."

"How come?" asked Andy.

"I just didn't feel like it," Amber said. "Besides, I heard they were moving Barry Dunn to ninth grade, too. That made me wonder. I think I'm better off here right now."

"I agree," Andy said with a dreamy look in his eyes.

"Come on, Andy." I gave his arm a tug and we continued toward the science wing.

When we got to Mr. Dirksen's lab, Josh in Principal Blanco's body was waiting for us.

"You ready?" I asked.

He nodded and straightened his suit. Meanwhile, Blanco in Josh's body hesitated. "I thought this invention had something to do with transferring intelligence."

"That's what it's *supposed* to do," I said.

"How many times have you used it to switch people's bodies before?" the principal in Josh's body asked.

My friends and I exchanged a nervous look.

"Uh, I think I'll take the Fifth Amendment," I said. "It's in the Bill of Rights, you know."

"Yes, of course," said Blanco in Josh's body. "The right to protect oneself against self-incrimination. I must say that you boys have demonstrated a deep understanding of your studies lately."

My friends and I shared a proud smile.

"So let's get on with it." Blanco in Josh's body sat down in one of the seats. Josh in the principal's body sat in the other. Andy and I stood behind the computer.

"Are you sure this will work?" Blanco in Josh asked.

"No sweat," I answered. "Everyone ready?"

Josh in Blanco and Blanco in Josh both nodded.

"Okay," I said. "One, two . . ."

Suddenly the door swung open. Barry Dunn stood there. His face was red, his hands were clenched into fists, and he was breathing hard.

26

Everyone froze. Barry stepped into the science lab. "Mr. Blanco?"

Josh in the principal's body didn't answer.

Barry frowned. "Hey, Mr. Blanco!"

Josh in Blanco's body still didn't answer. He was probably too busy preparing to be in his own body again.

"Hey, *Blanco*!" the principal in Josh's body shouted.

"Huh?" Josh blinked Blanco's eyes. "Oh, yeah, what do you want, Barry?"

Barry stepped closer. Everyone tensed. Barry held out his hand and reached toward our principal.

"I . . ." Barry began. "I just want to shake your hand."

Josh furrowed Blanco's brow. "Why?"

"Because you believed in me, Mr. Blanco." Barry grabbed the principal's hand and started to shake it. "When everyone else thought I had the brains of a street curb — "

"Speed bump," Andy corrected him.

"Yeah, whatever," Barry said and looked at our principal again. "You were the only one who had faith in me, Mr. Blanco. You were the only one who believed that I really am a lot smarter than I look. And I just want you to know that now that you skipped me ahead to ninth grade, I'm not gonna let you down. You're gonna be proud of me."

"Uh, right, sure, anything you say, Barry." Josh in Blanco's body shook Barry's hand.

"And now I gotta go home," Barry said. "I got an awful lot of homework to do tonight."

He went out the lab door.

"Barry Dunn rushing home to do homework?" muttered Principal Blanco in our friend's body. "Now I've seen everything!"

"Not really," replied Josh in the principal's body. "You've just seen an example of the kinds of things I could do if I were principal. I really think that after you give blood tomorrow morning you ought to consider switching with me again. I mean, I know I'm not very good at shaving, but otherwise I think I've proved that I'm a much better principal than you."

Blanco in Josh turned red and gritted his teeth. He turned to Andy and me. "I suggest you switch us fast, before I strangle him. I mean, before I strangle myself. I mean . . . Oh, whatever!"

"Here goes." I pushed the button.

Whump!

POSTSCRIPT

The next morning Andy and I picked up Josh and walked toward school. Now that he was in his own body again, he was back to wearing a sleeveless T-shirt and baggy shorts.

"How are you feeling?" I asked.

"Okay," Josh replied with a shrug.

"I can't believe you really wanted to stay in Blanco's body and be principal," Andy said.

"Hey, don't knock it until you've tried it," Josh replied.

"I guess it must be kind of cool to boss everyone around," I mused.

"Forget that," Andy said. "What's cool is to have your own office and get paid money to play computer games all day."

We got to school and went inside. Amanda Gluck came in behind us with Band-Aids all over her nose.

"Hey, Amanda, what happened to you?" Andy asked.

"I tried to shave my nostril hairs," she explained.

My friends and I winced. "You must've really wanted to come back to school."

"I have a right to a free education," Amanda replied. "And if I have to give up some nostril hairs, that's life. Now all I have to do is show Principal Blanco."

Amanda went down the hall toward the main office. At that moment, Ollie Hawkins came out of the office and trudged toward us with his head hanging.

"Hey, Ollie," I said. "What's wrong?"

"Principal Blanco just shot down the sports leagues for small guys," Ollie reported. "What a jerk. Yesterday he said yes; today it's no."

My friends and I shared a somber look. You couldn't help feeling bad for him.

"I have an idea," I said. "Maybe the school shot down your idea, but let's try petitioning the town recreation department. We'll help you."

Ollie straightened up and brightened. "You will? Great! I'll start a new petition right now!"

Ollie hurried down the hall. Just then Ms. Rogers turned the corner and strode past us as if she was in a hurry.

"Hey, Ms. Rogers!" Andy called.

She stopped and smiled at us. "Oh, hi, boys."

"What's the rush?" I asked.

"I have to go speak to Principal Blanco," she

said. "I just noticed the strangest thing. The door to my husband's lab is chained shut. I can't imagine why Principal Blanco would do that."

My friends and I shared a guilty look.

"Gee," I said. "I can't imagine why, either."

"Well, I'm going to find out," Ms. Rogers said as she pushed open the door to the main office and went in. "See you in homeroom, boys."

"So, how do you like that?" Andy said as we started toward homeroom. "Blanco must've locked the door so no one could use the DITS again."

"At least, not until Mr. Dirksen comes back from the Amazon," added Josh.

"Maybe it's just as well," said Josh. "Every time we use the DITS one of us gets in a lot of trouble."

"I guess you're right," Andy agreed.

It seemed as if they'd both forgotten about the mini-DITS, which was still in my locker. I decided not to remind them. You could never predict when it might come in handy.

ABOUT THE AUTHOR

Todd Strasser has written many award-winning novels for young and teenage readers. Among his best-known books are *Help! I'm Trapped in Obedience School* and *Abe Lincoln for Class President*. His most recent books for Scholastic are *Help! I'm Trapped in Obedience School Again* and *Help! I'm Trapped in an Alien's Body*.

Todd speaks frequently at schools about the craft of writing and conducts writing workshops for young people. He and his family live outside New York City with their yellow Labrador retriever, Mac.

You can find out more about Todd and his books at http://www.toddstrasser.com